D0496280

0060166649

BRING ME SUNSHINE

When marine biologist Jenny Payne agrees to spend Christmas working on the *Cape Adare* cruise ship, she envisions a few weeks of sunny climes, cocktails and bronzed men. But what she gets is an Antarctic expedition, extreme weather, and a couple of close shaves with death. And then she meets Kit Walker, the mysterious and handsome man who is renting the most luxurious cabin on the ship, but who nobody ever sees. Soon Jenny finds herself becoming increasingly obsessed with the enigmatic Kit, and the secrets he hides . . .

JANET GOVER

BRING ME SUNSHINE

Complete and Unabridged

LINFORD
Leicester

First published in Great Britain in 2013 by
Choc Lit Limited
Surrey

First Linford Edition
published 2018
by arrangement with
Choc Lit Limited
Surrey

A catalogue record for this book is available
from the British Library.

ISBN 978–1–4448–3684–4

Published by
F. A. Thorpe (Publishing)
Anstey, Leicestershire

Set by Words & Graphics Ltd.
Anstey, Leicestershire
Printed and bound in Great Britain by
T. J. International Ltd., Padstow, Cornwall

This book is printed on acid-free paper

This story is dedicated to
the man who taught me
about books and boats.
I'm back, Dad.

Acknowledgements

The idea for *Bring Me Sunshine* came from a journey made by my friend and sister-in-law. Mary Woodward, this book exists because of you. Thanks so much.

Before embarking on the fictional journey, I went on a real cruise. It was all research — honestly. Thanks to the wonderful people on board the Trollfjord for answering all my questions and letting me in on some of the stuff the passengers don't always get to see.

I also want to thank Clive and Maureen Willis for so generously sharing their experiences with me.

As always, my grateful thanks go out to my friends and fellow writers of the RNA who have always been there when I needed them. There are far too many of you to mention by name . . . but you know who you are and you know that I love you.

Thank you to the Choc Lit team who helped to make this the best book it could be. And also to the other authors who are friendly and supportive and such fun. It is a pleasure to be part of the family.

Last — but never least — my husband John, a tough and honest critic but always my strongest supporter. That's just one of the reasons I love you.

1

Two weeks before Christmas, Jenny Payne lost her lover, her job and her home all in one day.

It was not a good day, but it started well.

Jenny woke to a beautiful early summer morning. The sky was so blue it almost hurt to look at it. The sun was shining, but hadn't yet developed the energy-sapping heat that would come in the weeks ahead. Jenny threw herself through the shower and emerged clad in her favourite red cotton kimono. Grabbing some orange juice from the fridge, she stepped out onto the flat's tiny balcony, her short wet hair wrapped in a towel. As she sipped her juice, she looked out across the western Sydney suburbs, loving the green of the gum trees, interspersed with the brilliant purple of the Jacaranda flowers.

She always smiled when she saw the Jacarandas. When she was a student, the purple blooms had struck fear into her heart, signalling the approach of exams. Now she was a tutor, the Jacarandas meant the students were heading home, and she was free!

Jenny danced a few steps and twirled around; managing not to trip over the potted palms and Bougainvillea plants that almost filled the balcony. She downed the last of her juice and headed back into the kitchen and her brand new coffee machine.

Today she had time for coffee. She was in no hurry to get to her office at the university. In fact, she was pretty sure she wouldn't be going to work at all today . . .

'That's because today is THE day,' she told the African violet on the kitchen windowsill as she plugged in the coffee maker.

That's when the noise started. Sounds of enthusiastic lovemaking coming from the small flat's other bedroom. The bedroom where her sister Mandy slept, but seldom alone of late. This morning the noise, embarrassing though it might be, didn't bother her one bit. She wasn't jealous. Not anymore. In the past there had been moments — nights when Ray had failed to appear at her door as promised, mornings when she'd woken alone because Ray never spent the whole night with her. In those moments she had been jealous of Mandy and her boyfriend Peter. But not today, because everything was about to change!

The noise was getting a trifle loud.

'I think I'll have breakfast by the river,' Jenny told the house plants.

She ducked back into her room; to reappear a few minutes later dressed in a pair of faded jeans and a T-shirt that Ray had given her, a souvenir from one of his research trips to the Great Barrier Reef. Her hair was still wet, but it would dry soon enough. She would cycle down to the Lane Cove National Park, picking up coffee and an almond croissant from the new bakery on the way. Breakfast by the river was a great way to start the day and it would give Mandy and Pete the privacy they needed for the next hour or so. Jenny would be back in plenty of time to go and meet Ray. They were having lunch together at a tiny out-of-the-way restaurant that they both loved. There was a rather posh hotel nearby, and Jenny felt a tingle of pleasure at the thought that they might spend the afternoon there as they had a couple of times in the past. Even when they could make their relationship public, she'd still suggest they went there occasionally to recapture the thrill of those stolen hours in the luxury hotel suite.

She took her bike out of the garage it shared with Mandy's ancient blue Honda and set out. She had long ago mapped out all the possible routes to the National Park. It was one of her favourite places. She had never been there with Ray, but as soon as everything was out in the open, she'd take him there for a picnic. It would be so good to be free at last to do things like that.

As a professor, Ray had always been afraid to let the world know he loved a former student. He wasn't thinking of himself, of course. He was afraid Jenny would be hurt by the revelation. She had tried to tell him she didn't care, but he was firm. He didn't want her to take the risk.

It wouldn't be for much longer.

'Look out!'

The sudden loud blast of the car horn made her start and the bike's front wheel began to wobble. She clenched her fingers around the brakes and let one foot drop to the ground. The car she'd almost hit drove away, the driver's abrupt gesture out the window making his feelings abundantly clear. But today that didn't matter.

Jenny had never meant to fall in love with a professor, but that was before she walked into that packed lecture hall and saw him. Professor Ray Allen was handsome and erudite, with sparkling blue eyes and skin tanned to a golden sheen by his numerous ocean research voyages. There was much of Indiana Jones about Ray Allen — all he needed was a hat. He was everything her innocent and eager heart could possibly want. Sexy. Older — but not too old. Experienced. A little bit dangerous. There were times she was certain his eyes had rested on her a little longer than was absolutely necessary — and each time her heart beat just a little faster. As a student, Jenny had adored him from afar; safe in the knowledge that she was as unavailable to him as he was to her. All that changed when she graduated and joined the university as a tutor.

A teenage student was out of bounds, but a twenty-three-year-old fellow staff member was technically — well — not quite out of bounds.

For more than a year, nothing had happened, but then Jenny had changed the focus of the dissertation she was writing. She turned her attention to marine plants, and in turn Ray turned his attention to her. Jenny closed her eyes, remembering those heady weeks when she and Ray had discovered each other. Eyes meeting across the room. Hands touching as if by accident, as they worked in the tiny cubicles where science unravelled the secrets of the world. Tiny cubicles where she could almost feel his breath on her flesh as they worked. Almost hear his heart beating. Tiny cubicles where she lived out her romantic fairy tale.

They had fought it for a long time. Ray was afraid a relationship with him would taint Jenny's career. She was technically still a student, working towards her PhD. If it was known she was dating her professor . . . They had to wait, he told her, until she had her doctorate. But their feelings had been just too strong, and one wonderful afternoon, by unspoken agreement, they had both fled the university, and lost themselves in each other. They had been lovers now for a little over five months. Christmas was coming, and Jenny just knew that she and Ray were going to spend it together. Because everything was about to change.

'Today!' She wanted to shout it to the skies. It just had to be today. She had felt something different about Ray in these past couple of weeks. Now the lunch. This was going to be the best day of her life.

She leaped back aboard the bike, and turned off her usual route, heading for the bakery. She hadn't been there before, but a friend had recommended it. The friend was right. The bakery offered a mouth-watering selection of pastries. As today was a special day, Jenny weakened and bought an apricot Danish to go with her almond croissant. She wouldn't worry about the extra calories. But soon . . . she almost shivered with delight . . . soon she'd have to start being careful. There was a wedding dress in her future!

Jenny was so caught up in her

thoughts as she left the bakery, that for a few seconds she didn't recognise the car that pulled up across the road, at the gates of a very posh school. She did recognise the man who got out from behind the wheel. Ray! Her heart skipped a beat. He looked so handsome. Unusually for him, he was wearing a light linen jacket, with a shirt and tie. Of course! He had dressed especially for her. For today. Their day.

Jenny remained still for a few seconds more, just enjoying the sight of him. He walked around the car, with the casual, easy stride that always set her pulse racing. He opened the passenger's door and stepped back.

The woman wasn't particularly tall, or pretty, or even elegant. But she was familiar. Jenny had seen her at the university. Her father was the vice chancellor. She'd even been sitting next to Ray at one of the faculty dinners. Jenny had assumed it was just because of her father. Why then was Ray with her now?

On the other side of the road, Ray's arm was around the woman's shoulders in an almost possessive manner as he steered her towards the school. They paused at the gate. The woman put her hand protectively over her stomach in a manner that was universally recognised.

She was pregnant!

Ray kissed the woman tenderly, before they turned and walked into the school; the very picture of a happy couple planning a future for their child.

Jenny froze as a red hot arrow, shot from some invisible bow, tore through her.

Her chest was agony. She opened her mouth and gasped for air. Her legs were trembling. She had to get out of here in case he came back, but her feet seemed rooted to the ground. She looked down at her coffee cup. The steam rising from the hole in the plastic lid suggested it was hot enough to burn her hand, but the only pain she could feel was the pain in her chest. She looked about for a rubbish bin. Not seeing one, she simply placed the coffee and bag of breakfast on the ground. She wasn't a litter bug, but she just had to get away.

She forced her legs to move. One step at a time. She made it as far as the place where her bicycle leaned against a power pole. She gripped the handles as if she was drowning.

Ray and the vice chancellor's daughter? Whatever her name was? She couldn't believe it. And she was pregnant. Jenny knew she was jumping to conclusions — but it wasn't a very big jump. Deep inside she knew she was right. Pushing her bike, she started walking away from the brown croissant bag that lay on the pavement — looking as lost as her dreams.

How? Why?

When?

Oh God! Ray had slept with that woman at the same time as he had been with her . . . Jenny felt her gorge rising. Any minute now she was going to be physically sick.

A baby . . . A baby!

The words pounded in her head like a drumbeat. A baby. Somewhere in her dreams, Jenny had imagined a baby too. A baby with her own dark hair and Ray's blue eyes.

How had this happened? Ray loved her. She knew he did. Perhaps it was all a terrible mistake. A moment of weakness. A drunken one night stand . . . And now he was just doing the right thing.

As she groped frantically for excuses, Jenny knew deep in her heart of hearts, there was no excuse. Ray had cheated on her. And he had cheated on her with the woman who was . . . it hurt to even think the words . . . carrying his child.

He was a total bastard. A slime-ball and a prick!

Which made Jenny a victim. An innocent victim. A fool!

She pushed the bike into the road and swung herself aboard. Out of sheer habit, she turned in the direction of the university and set off, still in a shocked daze. Somehow she managed not to ride under a passing car and a short time later she arrived at the familiar and much-loved campus. She had barely dismounted from her bike, when she heard a voice calling from behind.

'Hey. Jenny. Heard the news about Professor Dreamy?'

It was another of the post grad students. A friend of sorts who had, during their undergrad days, shared both her college and her admiration for the Indiana Jones professor.

Jenny didn't reply. That was beyond her.

'He's going to marry the vice chancellor's daughter. What a loss to us all.'

Jenny's feet stopped moving for several seconds.

Marry?

With a supreme effort of will, Jenny kept moving. She mumbled something to her friend before making her excuses and hurrying away.

Why was she surprised? Of course he would marry the woman who was carrying his child. It was the honourable thing to do.

Ignoring the other voice in her head, the one with a tendency to call Ray rude names, Jenny walked in the direction of the tiny cubicle where she worked. On the way she had to pass Ray's much grander office. Knowing he wasn't there did not make it any easier. As she neared his door, her steps faltered. She wanted so much to go inside. To feel herself near him. To try to regain whatever she had felt yesterday. Or this morning. Before . . .

The door opened. The girl who walked out of Ray's office was tall and blonde, wearing a short denim skirt that showed every inch of her long legs. 'I was . . . just . . . looking for Ray. I mean, for Professor Allen . . . ' The girl blushed furiously as she stumbled over the words.

Jenny stood rock still and looked at the girl. She saw the embarrassment in the girl's flushed face. Saw the guilt in her eyes.

'I was just leaving my paper for him to look at,' the girl said, before hurrying away.

Jenny felt her legs start to tremble as the truth finally struck home with a force that could not be ignored.

What an idiot she'd been!

She put a hand out to steady herself against the wall. She knew that girl. Not her name or where she fitted into the university's hierarchy. She knew that girl because that girl was her . . . as she had been when Ray had first looked at her with those twinkling eyes and she had fallen for him. Fallen for a man who was obviously about to replace her with another woman. Fallen for a man who . . .

An image flashed into her mind. The school. Ray's fiancée. And that blonde girl? Was Ray already . . . ?

Self-loathing gave way to anger.

The bastard!

What had she been thinking? Ray wasn't in love with her. She was just another conquest. One more on what she suddenly realised was probably a very long list.

That unmitigated bastard!

Jenny felt a sudden surge of sympathy for the woman who even now was planning her future with a man who was a serial adulterer.

The total and unutterable prick!

Wrapping her anger around her like a protective blanket, Jenny made a beeline for the safety of her office.

If she hurried, she would be able to clear all her stuff out of there. She'd be gone by the time Ray got back. She could not — would not — face another day here. She never wanted to see him again. And if anyone ever found out that she . . . It was too horrible to contemplate. Better that she leave. Now.

Her office was about the size of a toilet, but that had never mattered. She loved working here. The research for her dissertation on the effect of heavy metal pollution on marine plants might not have been the stuff of most people's dreams, but to her, it was important. And so were her students. She loved teaching. Loved guiding them towards their degrees, as she had once been guided. Still, the semester was over. Her sudden disappearance wouldn't cause the students any problems. By the time they got back from holidays, someone new would have taken her place in the faculty.

With the door safely closed behind her, she started to pack. There wasn't much for her to take. She had taken her laptop home the night before, and it was still sitting in her flat. The piles of paper on her desk were mostly student essays she was marking . . . had been marking. They were almost finished. Someone else could easily take over. Maybe the girl who seemed to have already taken her place in Ray's . . . No, she pushed that thought aside. That was beneath her. Ray was beneath her, and all she felt for the girl was sympathy. She should go and warn her, but she wasn't that strong, and the girl wouldn't believe her. She took one final look around the office, lifted her framed degree from the wall, and walked out without a backward glance.

She was desperate to get to the sanctuary of home. Mandy was the only person who knew about Ray. She had disapproved from the start, but Mandy was her sister. Mandy would offer sympathy and support, a shoulder to cry on, and right now, she desperately needed that.

'Jenny! Look!' Mandy thrust her left hand under Jenny's nose before the door was even closed.

'What . . . ?'

'Pete and I are getting married!' The high-pitched squeal almost hurt her ears.

'Married . . . ?' Jenny forced her eyes to focus on the hand that Mandy was waving in front of her face. A thin gold band encircled the third finger, and a tiny diamond did its best to glitter.

'He made me breakfast in bed this morning, and when he brought the tray in — there was the ring. Isn't it gorgeous?'

'Yes. Gorgeous.' Jenny forced some enthusiasm into her voice.

'He's just so wonderful! I'm so happy!'

Mandy threw her arms around Jenny, who hugged her back. 'I'm really happy for you,' Jenny said, meaning it. She looked around for signs of her future brother-in-law, but he'd obviously gone to work.

'I want all my sisters to be bridesmaids. You will, won't you?' Mandy finally released Jenny from the bear hug.

'Of course I will.' Jenny walked the rest of the way into the flat. She dropped her things on the table and fixed a smile on her face. She was struggling to cope with this latest development. She had woken this morning thinking she was about to announce her engagement. Now she was alone — and it was Mandy planning to walk down the aisle.

19

Life was very cruel.

'I want a big church wedding. The full meringue dress. Lots of flowers.' Mandy was dancing around the room, her arms outspread. Then she suddenly stopped. 'Of course, that's going to cost a lot of money.'

Mandy, like Jenny, was a grad student and tutor, neither of which roles was exactly a gold mine. Their parents weren't wealthy either and had spent their money caring for a large family. Pete also worked at the university, and his faded jeans and battered old car were ample evidence of the state of his finances.

'That means we need to start saving right now.' Mandy, decidedly more sober-faced, dropped onto the couch and gestured to Jenny to sit with her.

'And . . . ?' Jenny asked.

'That's what I need talk to you about. Pete and I are going to move in together. It'll save on rent. Not that we don't want to live together anyway . . . I mean, we're getting married. And a white dress doesn't mean anything any-more . . . not really.' Mandy stumbled into silence.

Jenny put her hand on her sister's arm. 'Hey. That's fine. Of course you want to live together.'

'We thought . . . Well, this place is really great. But it is a bit small for three . . . and . . . ' Mandy stammered into silence.

'It's fine — don't give it a second thought. I'll find somewhere else to live. It's not a problem.'

'Really?' The high-pitched squeal was back. 'Oh, Jenny, you are my favourite sister.' Once more Jenny was enveloped in a bear hug. 'Of course, you don't have to move out right away. We know you'll need time to find somewhere else to live.'

'Don't worry about it,' Jenny said.

Mandy paused and looked carefully at Jenny's face. 'Are you sure? You don't look . . . '

'I'll be fine.' Jenny hastened to reaffix the smile on her face.

'Yes, you will. You always are.' Mandy abandoned her uncertainty and leaped to her feet. 'Anyway, I have to run. I'm meeting Pete for lunch and he's taking the afternoon off work so we can drive up the coast at tell Mum and Dad. We'll probably stay the night, so I'll see you tomorrow. Bye!'

The door clicked shut behind Mandy, and the room was suddenly very, very quiet.

Well, Jenny thought. The hat-trick. No job. No flat. No Ray. She let the full impact of that thought settle around her and waited for the tears.

No tears. Really. *No tears?* That wasn't right. Surely she should be weeping buckets. She'd just lost everything that mattered. Jenny took a deep breath and mentally sat back on her heels to examine herself and her situation.

All right — if she was to be perfectly honest, losing her flat wasn't really a problem. Flats were easy to come by — at least they were if you had a job.

Losing the job was a bit more serious, but she was a good teacher. She could always move to another university. Two weeks before Christmas wasn't the best time for job hunting. In the New Year — maybe then.

Losing Ray? That needed a bit more thought. Could she lose something she didn't actually have . . . and was never likely to have? She felt it then, a surge of emotion that caused her to drop to her knees on the carpet, her arms wrapped around her body. She was so angry. At Ray. At herself. So ashamed of her own naivety. She should have seen the signs. Ray's refusal to spend an entire night in her flat. His desire to keep their relationship secret. She might have a university degree, but when it came to men, she was a babe in the woods. It was the oldest story in the book. Innocent student seduced by worldly professor. Ray should be the one to lose his job. Not her. But people like Jenny were no real threat to the Professor Ray Allens of this world.

'You are a total shit, Ray Allen!' That helped, even if no one else could hear her. 'You don't deserve someone like me,' she added for good measure.

That was why there were no tears. She was too angry to cry.

At last Jenny slowly got to her feet. The clock on the kitchen wall said it was almost noon. Where had the time gone? About now Ray would be sitting at the restaurant, waiting for her. She had thought he was going to propose — but she was beginning to think he had planned to break up with her. Either way, it didn't matter now.

'He can just sit there!' she declared to the potted palm near the door. She wouldn't phone him. She grabbed the mobile phone out of her pocket and defiantly turned it off. That accomplished, she looked for something to do, just to keep her hands busy. If her hands were doing something else, they would not turn the phone back on.

She collected her watering can and began watering her plants.

'I deserve better than him,' she told the potted palm.

She pulled a few dying leaves off the aspidistra. 'If he could be unfaithful to his fiancée when she's pregnant — he would never be faithful to me,' she told it.

'I don't ever want to see him or hear from him again,' she explained to the begonia, as she ripped away the dying flowers.

'He was just using me!' The African violet suffered the full force of her sudden anger. Jenny looked at the spray of dirt across the kitchen.

'Sorry,' she told the plant as she scraped the dirt back in to the plastic pot and patted it down gently.

This was doing her no good at all. She needed something positive to do. She should start getting her life back on track.

'First up, I need a job,' she told the assembled flora. 'Preferably before I have to tell Mum and Dad that I've lost the last one.' Not that her parents would be angry. If she told them the

25

whole truth, they would be supportive. In many ways that would be even harder to deal with than somebody shouting at her might have been.

She opened her laptop.

The first thing she should do was resign her position at the university. That was a task she didn't relish. She quickly typed an e-mail, and hit the send key before she could change her mind. With the semester over, she didn't even need to give notice. It wasn't the way she wanted to leave, but right now, it was the only way.

Then she started looking at the job sites. Not one university in Australia or even New Zealand seemed in need of a marine biologist.

'And I'm not even sure I want to go back to uni right now,' she muttered to the plants. 'A change might be a good idea. But what can I do?'

She had a degree, but no real experience outside the university. Jenny modified her search words and clicked again.

There it was — the answer written in crisp clear pixels across her screen. It was perfect. It solved all her problems in one sun soaked moment.

All she had to do was make a few subtle changes to her CV.

'It's not lies,' she said to the room and its silent foliage. 'Not really. It's just . . . a shift in emphasis.'

She typed in her details, attached her modified CV and hit send.

2

Jenny was having another conversation with her plants next morning when the phone call came. She had spent the previous evening curled up on the sofa, with a glass of wine — well several glasses of wine — watching movies. Not weepy chick flicks, but thrillers with lots of gunfire and explosions and gory deaths. It had made her feel a lot better and there was a good chance most of the plants were going to survive her attentions this time.

Mandy hadn't come home last night. Jenny was glad of that. At some point she was going to have to tell her family what had happened. She could almost imagine the scene. Her father and oldest brothers would be all in favour of some rearrangement of Ray's face. Her mother would cope by making endless pots of tea and baking more cakes than even her large brood could possibly eat. Her eldest sister, Lisa, fancied herself a white witch, and would be casting spells, while her youngest brother, Mickey, would launch an internet campaign to expose Ray as an evil seducer of innocents. She was just telling the plants that she wanted to avoid all of that for as long as possible when the phone rang.

She sat looking at it for a few seconds. It couldn't be Ray. He only ever called on her mobile, which was still switched off.

'Hello.'

'Miss Payne? Ahh . . . Jenny Payne?' The voice sounded almost as if the speaker was ill.

'Yes . . . '

'Schofield here. Southern Cross Cruise Lines. You sent us your CV.'

'Yes. Yes. I did. Yesterday.' Jenny tried to keep the excitement out of her voice.

'Indeed. I have to ask you Miss Payne, when you would be able to start, if we were to . . . ahh . . . offer you a position?'

'I could start immediately.'

'Yes, well . . . ' the voice dripped disapproval, 'normally we would have gathered some references, and gone through a rigid interview process, but we find ourselves in something of a . . . ahh . . . dilemma.'

This was getting more and more interesting. 'What sort of dilemma?' she asked cautiously.

'Two of our expert lecturers have been taken ill with suspected salmonella.'

'Oh.' She didn't like the sound of that.

'No reflection on any of our vessels of course,' Mr Schofield continued. 'Something to do with children cooking at a school event.' He sounded as if he disapproved heartily of both children and schools.

'I understand.'

'The problem is that both were due to leave today on our new showpiece cruise. We might consider going with one less expedition lecturer, but we couldn't possibly go without two.'

'No. No. Of course not.' Jenny bit her lip, willing the man to talk faster.

'No . . . Unfortunately, none of our . . . ahh . . . existing crew are available on such short notice. They are all assigned to other expeditions. We need someone immediately.'

'I'm ready and willing to go!' she almost shouted down the phone.

There was a moment's silence. She bit her tongue and prayed.

'Yes, well. Ahh . . . This is most irregular. The ship sails this afternoon. You will, of course, need to pass an interview before we allow you on board.'

'Of course.' Jenny was practically jumping up and down on the spot.

'Yes . . . ' She could feel his hesitation. His uncertainty.

Please! Please! Jenny lifted her eyes to the heavens. This was perfect! A couple of weeks cruising the South

Pacific. Sun. Sand. Drinks with fruit and umbrellas in them. It solved the problem of a job and where to live all in one go. As for her former love life? Well, a tropical cruise was probably the best remedy for that as well.

'Where would you like me to come for the interview?' Jenny prompted, resisting the urge to add *ahh*. 'And at what time?'

'Circular Quay,' Schofield appeared to have made his decision. 'Two o'clock.'

'I can be there!'

'Very well. And Miss Payne, please bring your things with you. And your passport. If you are suitable, you will . . . ahh . . . need to board the *Cape Adare* immediately. She sails at four.'

'Yes, sir!' Jenny snapped to attention and saluted.

It didn't take long to pack. After all, she wouldn't need much. Swim suits. Shorts. Tank tops. She tossed in a couple of skirts and shirts. She probably needed to look a bit more professional when she was lecturing the passengers. But even so, no one got formal on a tropical cruise — did they? Then she thought of the captain's dinner. She'd sighed over Leonardo DiCaprio and Kate Winslet in *Titanic*. Not the iceberg bit — the elegant dinner. Ball gowns. Champagne. Dancing. She knew how it worked. She pulled out her best (only) cocktail dress — a sexy wisp of dove-grey silk and added that to the pile along with her five-inch Jimmy Choos (bought at a sale but still an extravagance she couldn't afford) and some underwear bought from a mail order catalogue. Underwear that she had never worn, because Ray . . .

No. She wouldn't go there.

As a concession to work, she tossed in a couple of books about marine mammals and ocean currents, not that she'd need them. She had a degree in marine biology. She wasn't going to have any trouble talking to a bunch of middle-aged cruise passengers about the lifecycle of the humpback whale. That was, of course, between long periods on a sun lounger with a cocktail in her hand as she sailed as far away from her old life as she possibly could.

She glanced at the phone and thought about calling her mother. She winced and decided against it. An e-mail would do just fine. She scribbled a quick note for Mandy, telling her not to expect to see her for a few days. That would do for now. She'd deal with the rest of her family if — when — she got the job. She could tell them everything from a safe distance. Walking out the door was difficult because she was wearing her rucksack and carrying both a suitcase and a laptop bag. Walking away was actually easier than she thought.

★　★　★

It shouldn't be called Circular Quay, Jenny thought as she lugged her things down from the overhead railway platform to ground level. There was

34

nothing circular about it. Sydney Cove was almost entirely square — from the walkway leading to the Opera House, to the ferry docks and the great ugly passenger ship terminal.

She weaved her way through the crowds of busy tourists and smiled at the aboriginal busker playing a didgeridoo. Overhead, the sun was shining. Some tanned teenagers were kicking a soccer ball around the lawns outside the Museum of Modern Art while children were buying ice cream from a vendor in a brilliantly coloured van. The water of Sydney harbour was a pleasing shade of blue, and the graceful arc of the Harbour Bridge was looking its picture postcard best. All the omens were right and Jenny was beginning to think she might just survive this day. Then the next, and maybe one day she'd find herself enjoying life again.

The ship was huge and exactly as she had imagined it. She stopped and stared. The top half was painted a blinding white. The lines of the hull sloped gracefully to the water. Even from this distance, she could see the lace curtains decorating the portholes. In fact, if she squinted, she could see a dining table set with silver cutlery and elegant long-stemmed wine glasses. A few passengers were leaning on the rails on the top deck. There would be a swimming pool there, she guessed. Deck chairs and a bar. There might even be handsome young men wearing bow ties serving drinks. It was the perfect remedy for her broken heart.

The cruise ship terminal was big and square and busy. Two tour buses were parked outside: one loading passengers, the other unloading them. Security men in bright green vests seemed more interested in sneaking outside to smoke cigarettes than giving directions. A tall wrought iron fence separated the public from the dock. On the other side of the fence, two fork lifts darted back and forth, loading pallets stacked with cardboard boxes through an opening in the side of the ship. Jenny checked out the labels on the boxes. Champagne. That was just the ticket. She would feel right at home on a ship that ordered champagne by the pallet-load.

Mr Schofield was short, round and grey, with a harassed frown on his pale face. Jenny had a feeling that expression was not caused by his urgent need to find crew for his ship. It looked permanent. He met her in the foyer of the terminal and showed her through to a small office.

'Thank you for coming on such short notice,' he said, the frown growing deeper. 'This is highly . . . ahh . . . irregular.'

'It's no problem at all,' she assured him.

The interview seemed the take forever. Mr Schofield must have read her CV in advance, but he went through it again, almost line by line. Then he pulled out the cruise company's rule book for another line by line review. Jenny was hard put to pay attention, when just outside the window, she could see passengers starting to board the ship. She just wanted to walk up that gangplank and sail away to somewhere with sun and surf and single men — honest single men.

'Have you got any questions, Miss Payne?' Schofield dragged her back from her daydreams.

'No. You've explained it all quite clearly,' she said.

Schofield frowned. Had she missed something important?

'Very well. As I said, this is highly irregular . . . If it wasn't something of an emergency . . . ahh . . . '

'I understand totally,' Jenny hastened to reassure him. Now she was this close, she wanted that job more than anything else in the world.

'Yes . . . ' Schofield shrugged in a resigned fashion and pushed some documents towards her. 'If you'll just sign these . . . '

Jenny had a quick glance at the contents. There seemed to be an employment agreement and something that looked like insurance. She signed and slipped her copies into her rucksack.

'Can I go on board now?'

'Ahh . . . '

Schofield looked as if he was searching for a reason to say no. When he couldn't find one, he nodded, and slipped his papers back into his briefcase, which he took with him as he escorted Jenny through the terminal. She showed her passport to a uniformed officer at the gate and turned towards the gangway.

'No, Miss Payne. Not that way.'

'Sorry?' Jenny looked the full length of the ship. Unless they expected her to jump, the gangway was the only way on board.

'That's not the *Cape Adare*.'

She looked up at the name painted on the graciously curved hull. He was right. 'Then where . . . ?'

Schofield indicated that she should follow him as he walked away from the cruise ship towards the far end of the dock which was noticeably bare of anything resembling a ship of any kind. Was she expected to swim?

'Seaman Brown will take you to the *Adare*.'

Jenny stopped a few centimetres short of the edge and looked down. Some sort of inflatable boat sat bobbing in the water about a metre below. A young man in a uniform was grinning up at her.

'Umm . . .'

'The *Adare* has been undergoing a refit. We are not taking passengers on board here in Sydney, so she is docked in . . . ahh . . . White Bay. It's just a few minutes away.'

'Oh.'

'Just toss your stuff down,' Seaman Brown called.

Jenny shrugged and did what she was told. She spotted some concrete steps leading down to the water. They were wet and looked very slippery, but they seemed her only option. She dropped onto a small bench seat that crossed the middle of the boat, and gripped the edge tightly. This probably wasn't the right time to say that she wasn't very keen on small boats.

'This won't take long,' Brown said as the engine roared to life under his hand.

The little rubber boat surged forward with startling speed. Jenny almost lost her seat. Only the tenacity of her death-like grip kept her upright. The boat powered towards the Harbour Bridge, leaping and bucking like some wild horse with every ripple on the water. As they sped under the bridge, Jenny did not even have time to admire the impressive structure. She kept her eyes firmly fixed on the floor of the boat. If she was to lose her seat — she was aiming to land on the floor, not in the water.

'There she is.'

Jenny kept her fingers locked on the seat, but looked up to follow the seaman's pointing figure.

'That little boat is the *Cape Adare*?'

'Not so little.' He appeared affronted. 'She's eleven thousand tonnes.'

Jenny had no idea what that meant, but she did know the ship they were approaching was a lot smaller than the one they'd left behind. It looked very small to be tackling the Pacific Ocean — but she couldn't argue. The name *Cape Adare* was painted in large letters along her side.

'She's just been refitted for these special trips,' Brown continued as he eased back on the throttle. 'There won't be a lot of passengers on board. Not a lot can afford what she's offering.'

That sounded better. If this was the sort of ship that attracted rich people, then it sounded pretty attractive to Jenny as well. The inflatable began to move into the ship's shadow. Jenny admitted that up close, it was bigger than she had originally thought. But . . .

'Aren't we going to the dock?' she asked.

'No. This Zodiac has to go back on

board, so I figured you may as well ride it up with me. You'll have to do it sooner or later.'

'Ride it up?' She didn't like the sound of that.

The seaman pointed upwards. Slowly Jenny tilted her head. High above her, some sort of gantry was protruding from the side of the ship.

'You don't mean . . . ?'

'Why not?'

The seaman signalled to someone above, and Jenny heard the whir of a winch. No. No. She wasn't doing this. How could she ever have thought the ship was small? That great iron hull was the size of a ten-storey building. At least. Maybe twenty. She wasn't going to get winched up there in some blow-up rubber dinghy.

Seaman Brown stood up and started moving around the boat, which rocked alarmingly. Jenny bit her lip. She was not going to make a fool of herself. Not yet, anyway. In a matter of seconds, Brown had clipped four rather thin-looking wire ropes to the corners of the boat.

'Here we go.'

The earth moved — or rather, the boat moved. It broke free of the water and began to ascend, passing the portholes with alarming speed. Jenny wanted to close her eyes, but was afraid that would be even more frightening. She kept her gaze fixed on the floor of the Zodiac. With a jerk, the boat stopped moving. Jenny cast a quick sideways glance at Brown, who seemed totally unconcerned by the sudden pause in their ascent.

'Out you go,' he said cheerfully.

Out? Jenny looked around. The boat was dangling over the water next to the open deck of the ship. Two men were looking at her expectantly.

'What about my bags?' As a delaying tactic, it wasn't much, but it was all she could think of in a hurry.

'I'll take care of those.'

There was nothing for it but to do as she was bid. Jenny slid tentatively towards the edge of the Zodiac, her fingers still gripping the seat with every ounce of strength she possessed. As she did, one of the seamen on board the ship opened a gate in the deck rail. That was an improvement. At least she had nothing to climb over. Now all she had to deal with was the gap between the boat and the ship — the gaping chasm that led down to the water several kilometres below.

'Take my hand.'

A hand the size of a bear's paw was reaching for her. She gripped it like her life depended on it — which it probably did. Slowly she straightened her legs then, with a sudden rush, she almost leaped out of the inflatable boat, onto the comfortingly solid iron deck.

The bear-like paw held her hand for a moment longer, shaking it. 'Welcome aboard!' His voice was as big and powerful as he was. 'I'm really glad you could make it. I'm Karl Anders, the expedition leader.'

As Jenny's heart rate began to return

to something approaching normal, she noticed that the rest of Karl was as bear-like as his hand. He had masses of curly rust-coloured hair with just a touch of grey, a beard that several birds could nest in and he towered over her.

'I'm pleased to meet you,' Jenny said as she regained the power of speech. Behind her, the Zodiac was being swung onto the deck, bringing Seaman Brown and her bags with it.

'We were a bit worried that we'd have to go without you. That would have been a shame. It's going to be a great trip. We are expecting spectacular weather. Sunshine all the way.' Karl was the friendliest and most cheerful bear she'd ever met.

'That's great . . . '

'First up, let's get you settled in,' Karl continued before she could get a word in edgeways. 'You're with the rest of the expedition team. Deck Two Port side. 213.' He handed her a piece of white plastic about the size of a credit card.

'Yes. Right.' Jenny bent to pick up her things.

'You'll meet the rest of the team a bit later. My wife Anna will kit you out. We're meeting in the theatre after we clear the harbour. Brown, would you help Jenny with her bags.' Karl gave the young seaman a slap on the back that would have felled a decent sized gum tree.

'Yes, sir!' Brown said quickly. Jenny caught a flash of what she thought was a wink as the young sailor hefted her rucksack and bag. 'Follow me.'

She grabbed her laptop bag and hurried after him, wondering what was involved in being 'kitted out'.

They made their way along a covered walkway. To her left, a lifeboat hung in a gantry. Before she could get her bearings, Brown pushed open some heavy glass doors leading to the interior of the ship. Jenny followed him into a world of gleaming wood and thick plush carpets.

'This is deck six,' Brown explained.

'There are lifts and stairs forward.'

He led Jenny to the stairs and began to descend further into the ship, her bags in no way slowing him down.

Jenny hurried after him, too intent on keeping her feet on the stairs and her laptop on her shoulder to pay much attention to her surroundings, other than to note the muted colours, polished wood and large framed photos of ships and seascapes. The company must run a lot of cruises to different places, she thought as she passed a brilliant green photo of the Northern Lights.

Four floors down, the stairs ended in a tiny, plain lobby. No carpet here, just serviceable rubber floor. The sign on one of the doors said 'Sick Bay'. Another said 'Crew Only'.

'The security code is C8576X,' Brown said as he tapped it into the keypad lock on the door.

'C85 . . . '

' . . . 76X, that's right.' Brown swung the heavy metal door open and Jenny followed him through.

In the crew quarters, the framed photos gave way to cork notice boards covered with postcards and snapshots, notices and computer printouts. Through an open doorway, Jenny saw a few people were sitting at tables in some sort of a common room. They looked up and smiled in a welcoming fashion. Jenny barely had time to nod back, before she had to hurry on after Brown.

'Ward room,' the seaman said. 'Through there is the kitchen. We've got internet access for the expedition team down here and some recreational facilities. TV and so on.'

'There's not much room,' Jenny noted as she followed Brown down a narrow corridor, with a very sturdy-looking hand rail bolted to one side.

'Depends on your viewpoint,' Brown said. 'Right, here you are, 213. Easy to find — remember the odd numbers are down the port side.'

'And the port side is . . . '

Brown looked at her and raised an eyebrow. 'Left.'

'Yes. Yes. Left. Of course,' Jenny tried not to let her embarrassment show. She stood there, uncertain of what to do next.

'The key,' Brown suggested.

'The key!' Jenny dug into her pocket and retrieved the small rectangle of plastic. She slid it into the lock and pushed the door. It barely moved.

'The doors are a bit heavy until you get used to them,' Brown offered.

Jenny pushed even harder. The door swung inwards and revealed her new home.

The cabin was long and narrow. A single bunk lined the far wall below a small round porthole. To her right, just inside the door, was a walled cubicle that she assumed was a toilet. It was about the right size. There was a small desk and a couple of very small cupboards for storage.

'Here you go.' Brown dropped her

bag. 'See you later.' He grinned and was gone.

It's green, Jenny thought as she stood there, too stunned to move. Pastel, insipid, pale green. She hated pale green, but if the colour of her cabin was the worst thing to happen to her today, it would be one hell of an improvement on yesterday.

She stepped a little further into the cabin, and tentatively opened the cubicle door. Not only did it contain a toilet, there was also a shower, hand basin and a wall-mounted cabinet to hold a toothbrush and bar of soap. A very small bar of soap. Stepping back out of the cubicle, Jenny examined the rest of her quarters and found the same theme. Space was obviously at a premium on board a ship.

'Not that it matters,' she said out loud as she threw her things into the drawers, 'I'll be on deck most of the time, enjoying the sunshine. Swimming in the pool . . . or taking passengers on snorkelling expeditions on the coral reefs.' That sounded better.

Jenny slid her empty bags under her bunk, and then kneeled on the bedcovers to peer through the small porthole. Just a few centimetres below the glass, the waters of Sydney Harbour flowed past. Flowed? They were moving? Jenny stood still, and concentrated, but there was no sensation of movement at all. Turning she left the cabin and retraced her route to the deck. She did not see another soul until she emerged through what she thought were the same glass doors onto the covered deck. The ship's rail was dotted with people, taking in the spectacular sight of Sydney Harbour as it passed in front of them.

Jenny made her way along the deck, to a place near the back of the ship, where she could be alone. Now that she was underway, she was starting to have second thoughts. She was on board a ship, with dozens, maybe even hundreds of people crowded in together. Why then was she starting to feel lonely?

Either side of the ship, the bays and beaches of Sydney Harbour were slipping past. Behind them, the afternoon sun glinted on the windows of houses where families would soon be settling down to their evening meal. In the restaurants and nightclubs, friends and lovers would come together — to celebrate a special event, or just to share the day's experiences.

Somewhere, would Ray be sitting down to dinner with his fiancée? She thought the word slowly and with great care, as if to reinforce its meaning. Maybe talking about the baby. Discussing names and what colour to paint the nursery. Jenny slipped her hand into her pocket and pulled out her mobile phone. Would there be mobile services in the middle of the ocean? She should just check while she was in range. She turned the phone on and waited as it connected to her network. Three missed calls. Mandy. Her mother. Her mother again. Two text messages. Mandy wanting to know where she was and a later one also from Mandy, having read her note, telling her to have a great time. That gave her just a twinge of guilt. She hadn't exactly lied in the note she had left for her sister, but she had hinted her abrupt departure was more in the nature of a last minute holiday.

Nothing from Ray. Not even a call to find out why she hadn't met him for lunch. Maybe he was just relieved that she'd stood him up. Or had she stood him up? Maybe he hadn't even been going to keep their date. Maybe he hadn't even given a single thought to her sudden disappearance. She snapped the phone shut, and for an instant contemplated hurling it overboard. She didn't. It was an expensive phone, and besides, as a marine biologist, she didn't approve of littering the harbour.

The seagulls wheeled, screaming around the ship's wake, dipping into the water in search of food. How mournful they sounded. How lonely they made her feel, standing at the rail. She was on a ship full of total strangers.

Only two people knew her name — and she couldn't even say the reverse. She had no idea what Seaman Brown's first name was — assuming he had one. All her life, she'd been surrounded by people. Her huge family. Friends. Fellow students. Now she was totally alone. More alone than she had ever been before. She would be alone for the next three weeks. She watched the white water of the ship's wake, wondering if she had made a terrible mistake quitting her job so quickly. Maybe she should have waited.

The *Cape Adare* slipped between Sydney Heads, heading for the Pacific Ocean. Jenny looked up at the great stone cliffs as they were left behind. For one heart-stopping moment, as the ship changed direction, the two rock walls seemed to meet, forming a dark sullen barrier cutting her off from her family, her friends, Ray . . . everything and everyone she knew. Leaving her outside. Stranded. Alone . . .

'Oh, stop it!'

What was she thinking? She had finally seen Ray's true colours. He wasn't going to change. Her family and her real friends would still be there when she got back. She was going to miss Christmas dinner with her family, but there was nothing wrong with that. She was sailing forth on an adventure. Heading for the sunny South Pacific islands. Sun. Surf. Maybe even some good old-fashioned holiday sex. She was going to have a ball!

'Anyway — it's too late to go back,' she told the circling gulls. 'I'd have to swim.'

The swimming would have to wait until the ship got into warmer waters a bit further north.

North . . .

North?

Jenny watched the coastline moving past, a couple of kilometres away, down the ship's right side. The starboard side. Wouldn't that mean they were heading south?

She took a step away from the rail.

An image began to form in her mind, several images. She almost ran along the deck to the glass doors and into the foyer. The huge framed photo was still there. The green curtain hanging in a dark star littered sky. She read the small bronze name plate. The Aurora Australis. The southern lights. Southern. Visible from the Southern Ocean and nowhere else on the planet.

She darted down the stairs to the next framed photograph.

A ship. Mirror-like blue water and . . . icebergs.

Down another floor. Penguins stared back at her from the photo frame.

'I've got a bad feeling about this,' she told them. A detailed plan of the ship hung on the opposite wall. She consulted it quickly. The lecture theatre was on deck five. She set off back up the stairs.

When she entered the lecture theatre at a stumbling run, she didn't notice the plush seats, some of which were occupied. She didn't notice the heads turning her way and she certainly didn't notice the dignified grey-haired gentleman in uniform standing on the podium. All she saw was the image on the projector screen. The ship. THIS ship. Surrounded by icebergs. The banner said 'Antarctic Expedition'.

'Oh, shit!'

3

The silence in the room was almost tangible. It curled around Jenny's words as if to highlight the expletive in glowing neon. On the podium, the dignified gentleman in uniform slowly raised his eyebrows. Somewhere in the room, a girl sniggered. Jenny began to hope for an iceberg. Or a tidal wave. Anything to direct everyone's attention away from her.

'I'm sorry . . . ' Should she call him Sir? There was enough gold braid on his uniform to finance several small African countries. Jenny guessed that made him the captain.

'Glad you could join us, Jenny.' Rising like a leviathan from the depths of her embarrassment, Karl Anders stepped to the front of the podium. 'Captain, this is Jenny Payne. Our new expedition specialist in marine biology.

Jenny, meet Captain Haugen.'

'Captain Haugen.' Jenny felt an overwhelming urge to salute.

'Jenny,' the captain smiled at her. 'Welcome aboard the *Cape Adare*.' His accent, as much as his name, betrayed his Scandinavian origins.

'Thank you, sir.'

'You can meet the rest of the team later,' Karl offered. 'If you'd like to take a seat . . . '

Jenny dropped into the semi-anonymity of the nearest seat. She slid as far down into it as she could; hunching her shoulders against the eyes she could feel staring at her.

'As I was saying,' the captain continued, 'we'll be using the next couple of days as shake-down before taking on passengers in Hobart. Each of you will be shown your assignments for the emergency drills. I believe most of you are experienced at this, so I don't imagine there will be any problems.'

No problems except of course that they were going in the wrong direction.

How could this have happened? Jenny ran her conversation with Mr Schofield through her head. True, her mind had wandered a bit, but at no point did she recall the word Antarctica being spoken. It was equally true that no one had mentioned tropical islands either, but wasn't that where all cruise ships went?

Apparently not.

Jenny sank even further into her seat, her eyes firmly fixed on the floor.

So much for her visions of bikini clad sunbathing. That particular item of clothing was going to remain buried in the back of her drawer. There wouldn't be much call for it where she was going. Jenny's heart fluttered in a moment of panic. What was she going to wear? She didn't know much about Antarctica, but she did know that even in summer the temperatures rarely got above freezing.

Icebergs. Freezing temperatures. That was not what she'd signed up for. Who would want that?

A pair of shiny black shoes appeared in the few square centimetres of floor she was gazing at. They stopped, apparently waiting for something. Slowly she uncurled herself and raised her eyes to find the captain looking down at her. This close, his lined face told of many, many years' exposure to sun and wind, and he had an aura of quiet competence. This was a man who you could trust with your life at sea. His pale blue eyes were surrounded by deep laugh lines. At least she hoped they were laugh lines.

Jenny leaped to her feet. She almost snapped to attention. Something about the captain just inspired that sort of reaction.

'I understand this is your first expedition, Miss Payne,' he said.

'That's right, sir.'

'I'm sure you'll do just fine. We're not a big ship, but we like to think we are the best.'

'Yes. Sir.' At some point, she would have to say something else.

'Fine. Carry on.' The captain strode up the aisle, nodding to a few people scattered among the seats, then left the theatre.

'Now — down to business.' Karl had stepped onto the podium. 'Has everyone got their schedules?'

She seemed to be the only one not clutching a sheaf of papers. Tentatively she raised her hand. A few seconds later, a folder was passed back from the front row. Jenny opened it and inspected the first page.

Cape Adare — Inaugural Antarctic Expedition.

She shuddered again and quickly turned the page to find a map of their route. There it was. Antarctica. A great white mass at the bottom of the page. She tried to reassemble what she knew about it. Penguins and seals. Humpback whales and krill. Dead explorers. Lots and lots of snow and ice. That seemed to sum it up. Not her idea of a good time. Not at all.

Was it too late to get out of this?

The dining area was crowded, but Jenny had never felt so alone. She did not know the name of a single person in the room, which was not surprising considering she had only been introduced to three people on board the ship. She doubted the captain dined with the crew, Karl wasn't here and Seaman Brown was probably off doing whatever it was that seamen do when they are not terrifying people in a blow-up rubber dinghy. All the other people in the room seemed to know everyone else. Friends were laughing together. Conversations buzzed around the dining tables, punctuated by greetings to newcomers.

An overwhelming sense of loneliness and isolation threatened to knock Jenny's feet from under her.

If she didn't know anyone, then the reverse was also true. Everyone here might know her name, particularly after her spectacular entrance into the theatre, but they didn't know her. No one knew where she came from. Or about the huge family that had always been her support and comfort. No one knew that she loved eating baked beans on toast in front of romantic films. No one knew that her flat was slowly being overgrown by potted plants. No one knew about Ray. There was no one to whisper a secret to. No one to share a memory with. No shoulder to cry on.

There was no one who knew or cared one toss about Jenny Payne.

On the other side of the room, a woman noticed her. She said something to her companions at the table and five pairs of eyes turned towards Jenny. That was enough for her. She turned and walked out of the room. She wasn't hungry anyway. She headed back towards the sanctuary of her cabin, but heard voices further along the corridor. More old friends catching up after some time apart. She ducked through the door into the lift lobby, feeling a sense of relief as the door shut behind her. Without giving any real thought to where she was going, Jenny hit the top button. The glass sided box moved slowly up through the decks, giving her tantalising glimpses of polished chrome and timber, and empty spaces.

The lift stopped on the seventh floor. Jenny stepped out into the lobby. Behind her was the passenger's bar, with huge windows and glass walls to provide spectacular views. During the voyage, this would no doubt be the social centre of the ship, where passengers would swap tales of their adventures while drinking beer and cocktails. With no passengers yet on board it was in semi darkness — gloomy and depressing and even more claustrophobic than the crowded crew quarters.

Jenny headed for the outside deck. She pushed the glass door, but her hand slipped off the handle, rapping her knuckles painfully on the metal frame.

God, that thing was heavy. What was it with doors on this ship? Did the designers not want them to be opened?

Jenny tried again. This time she put her weight behind it and the door swung open a bit too fast. She almost fell through the opening onto the deck outside. A set of steep metal steps led up to the lobby roof. Without a moment's thought, Jenny climbed them . . . and stepped out among the stars.

It was like nothing she had ever seen before.

The sky was inky black, patterned by great clusters of stars. More stars than she had ever seen in her life. They were so thick they almost looked like clouds. Shiny, glowing clouds. She spun slowly, her face turned to the heavens and the distant suns twinkled and danced around her like she had stepped into a fairy tale. Any minute now, angels would appear to dance with her . . .

. . . but they had better have very strong wings.

Jenny was suddenly aware of the wind trying to blow the clothes from her body. The wind, strengthened by the speed of the ship was almost enough to chill her, despite the warmth of the evening. She moved forward, where a sloping glass wall offered protection from the wind. She turned and looked back. The ship's funnel rose behind her, a spotlight picking out the cruise line logo on its side. Southern Cross Cruises. She lifted her face to the sky again and found the constellation, the stars brighter than any others. It really was quite beautiful.

Jenny felt her spirits lifting. Wasn't this what she had wanted? To get away from everything. If she was among strangers, at least no one knew about Ray. No one knew what a fool she had been to fall for someone like him. Jenny closed her eyes as tears threatened.

No.

She opened her eyes again, blaming the tears running down the side of her nose on the wind, not on her emotions. She shook her head. She was not going to be like that. This was an adventure. It wasn't what she had expected, but it might be fun. OK — it was going to be cold, but cold could be fun too. Couldn't it? And anyway, she suddenly remembered her conversation with Mr Schofield. They were stopping in Hobart in two days to pick up their passengers. If she really hated it, she could always jump ship. They didn't hang you for desertion from a cruise ship . . . did they?

Jenny smiled and ran the back of her hand over her nose, which was also feeling the effects of the cold wind and made a note to herself to bring a tissue next time she came up here. Then she noticed the structure at the rear of the observation deck. She cast her mind back to the plan of the ship that she had studied earlier. The structure housed a sauna. One with a view. Intrigued, Jenny decided to investigate.

The sauna was on a raised section of the deck at the very rear of the observation platform. Steps led up to the doors, marked male and female. A narrow access path led around the edge of the structure, but a gate blocked the path and the sign said crew only. Well, she was crew, wasn't she? There would be a lovely view of the back of the ship and the white trail it left in the sea. She could go back there and bid a symbolic farewell to her old life. That was just what she needed. The gate wasn't locked. Jenny tugged at the latch until it slipped open. With one hand on the metal deck railings, she made her way down the side of the sauna. To her left was a huge glass wall, and Jenny realised that was the picture window that allowed people in the sauna to look out. Positioned as it was on the side of the ship, no one would see in, except for someone on this tiny walkway. The sauna was in darkness. Jenny continued around the back of the structure. The walkway here looked down on the open deck below, which explained why the sauna wall was solid. No voyeurs here — just voyagers. Jenny chuckled at her own pun, and then out of curiosity peeked around the far corner of the sauna.

The man was naked. And hot — in more ways than one.

He was sitting on the wooden bench inside the sauna, facing the glass wall and the darkness beyond. His arms were spread across the back of the bench as he leaned back against the wall, his eyes shut. His well-muscled chest was damp with sweat, as was his dark hair. He looked like something out of the sort of dream you never told anyone about.

Jenny gasped and took half a step back into the shadows. The sauna certainly did have a view — but probably not the one the designers had intended. She turned to sneak away, but stopped. She could no more walk away than she could swim back to Sydney. She just had to have a second look.

Slowly she stepped forward, and peeked.

His body was firm and muscular. Jenny guessed he spent time in the gym as well as the sauna. His chest was broad, with a light smattering of dark hair that faded down across the six pack of his stomach towards his hips. His legs seemed to go on forever. Only the condensation on the inside of the glass preserved his modesty. Jenny wished she could wipe it away.

As for his face.

Handsome wasn't the right word. A lot of men are handsome. She had once thought Ray was handsome, but Ray had never made her breath catch in her throat like this. No one had. She could have looked at that face for hours. It was like a work of art. Beautiful, but powerful too, framed by longish wavy dark hair. Her fingers ached to touch the line of his jaw, to trace the sinews of his neck to the place where the pulse beat at its base. To feel his heart beating.

He moved, slowly stretching his muscles, as if to ease stiff joints. Then he opened his eyes.

Jenny gasped and ducked back into

the shadows. Had he seen her? How embarrassing, to be caught staring in the window like some peeping Tom . . . or Thomasina. Jenny heard a noise inside the structure, and risked another quick peek around the corner. The sauna was dark — and now empty. The gorgeous occupant was no doubt in the locker room, putting on his clothes ready to re-join the rest of the crew.

This raised an interesting point. Was he crew? There were no passengers on board — so he must be. But crew were not permitted to use the sauna. That was one of the rules she'd read in the paperwork Karl had handed her earlier today. Maybe the rules didn't apply when there were no passengers on board?

Before she could follow that thought, Jenny heard the sauna's outer door open. The man emerged, dressed in jeans and a black T-shirt that was damp enough to cling to his shoulders in a most appealing way. He walked across the open deck towards the stairs, seemingly unaware of Jenny peeking around the corner of the sauna. As soon as he vanished down the stairs, Jenny left her hiding place. Silently, she too walked to the stairs and peered down. There was no sign of her quarry — so she began to descend. She stopped at the next deck. The bar was still in darkness. She doubted he would be heading for the gym or the Jacuzzi — so she continued cautiously down the stairs.

Deck six was the first of the passenger accommodation decks. A corridor led forward, past a few cabins to the restricted area where the senior officers lived, and to the bridge. Towards the rear of the ship, the cabins became larger, more luxurious and more expensive, culminating in the Australis Suite — otherwise known as the owner's cabin. Jenny had noticed it on the ship's plan. It was at least five times the size of the other passenger cabins and probably ten times the size of the shoebox where she was living. She peered cautiously down the corridor and there he was, striding confidently towards the rear of the ship.

The figure turned the corner and was gone, presumably into the owner's suite.

Was that the ship's owner? Surely not. He was so young and gorgeous. Outside the pages of romance novels, weren't shipping tycoons old men with more chins than eyebrows? If he wasn't the owner, and couldn't be a passenger — was he crew? Maybe he was a stowaway.

Jenny hesitated. She certainly wasn't about to go knock on his door and ask him if he was a stowaway, and mention that, by the way, he looked good naked.

'Here you are!'

Jenny jumped and spun around to face the voice. A woman was coming up the stairs towards her. It was the same woman who had noticed her down in the crew dining room.

'Hello . . . ' Jenny said.

'I'm Anna. Karl's wife,' the woman said.

Jenny had to struggle to keep a straight face. Anna was probably about thirty, with friendly brown eyes and hair in a long ponytail. She was also incredibly tiny. She would barely come half way up Karl's chest. Jenny bit back a giggle.

'I tried to catch your attention at dinner,' Anna continued. 'I know you're new. I'm the ship's nurse — but most of the time I'm not very busy, so I'm also sort of the mother hen for the new girls.'

Mother hen sounded incongruous coming from a woman who barely came past Jenny's own shoulder, but Anna's face was kind, and Jenny realised that right now, she could use a friend.

'Nice to meet you,' she said.

'You're going to need uniforms and wet weather gear. Not to mention gear for when you're on the ice,' Anna said. 'I can sort that out for you.'

'Great!' On the ice didn't sound too good, but despite that, Jenny felt a wave of relief. At least she wouldn't freeze to death.

'Why don't you come downstairs to the mess for coffee and meet some people.' Anna's smile suggested she understood why Jenny had fled the dining area earlier.

'That would be nice.'

'We've got it pretty easy as there are no passengers on board, so we're all sitting around and catching up. You'd get a chance to meet everyone.'

'I'd like that . . . ' Jenny hesitated. 'I know there's not supposed to be passengers — so who is the man in the owner's suite?'

'How do you know about him?' Anna looked surprised. 'You talked to him?'

'No. No. I just saw him . . . ' Jenny almost blushed, 'walking down the corridor there. I wondered who he was.'

'He is a passenger,' Anna said in a conspiratorial whisper. 'The only one we have. Some special deal to let him on board early. No one has seen him except the stewards who took him dinner in his cabin tonight. No one knows who he is, but we've been told to treat him with kid gloves.'

'Oh.'

'Exactly,' said Anna, a huge grin spreading across her face. 'Anyway, that's enough with our mysterious passenger. I'm sure we'll find out eventually. In the meantime, come on. We can grab some coffee and chat.'

'That sounds great.' Jenny followed Anna as she headed back to the stairwell. She descended a couple of steps, then peered back down the corridor. There was nothing to see.

4

'You are going to drown. You know that, don't you?'

Jenny looked down at the crumpled mass of orange fabric on the deck. 'Right at this moment, that doesn't seem to be a bad idea at all.'

The man beside her started to laugh. 'Come on, try again. It's not rocket science, you know.'

'Rocket science I could manage . . . but that thing.'

Karl laughed as he picked up the life jacket and thrust it back at Jenny. She sighed, and turned the jacket the right way up.

'What happened to the good old slip-it-over-you-head-and-tie-the-tapes life jackets?' she asked as she pulled the orange fabric hood the right way out.

'Cold water. You need a bit more protection.'

Jenny slipped her arms into the life jacket that looked more like a strait-jacket. This time, she got it right.

'Fine,' Karl said. 'Now, as you're new, your lifeboat station will be here. Nothing too complex. Just helping the passengers with their life jackets.'

Here was on deck six, starboard side, on the covered walkway next to the lifeboat. The Zodiac that had given Jenny such a terrifying ride up the ship's hull nestled just behind the bigger boat. The actual boats would be operated by ship's crew like Seaman Brown. They were the professionals. They ran the ship. Then there were the expedition crew. People like her. Expedition crew worked with the passengers — giving lectures, taking them on shore excursions and generally keeping them entertained and out of trouble. The third group in the on-board hierarchy was the hotel staff who were responsible for feeding and housing both passengers and crew. Once the passengers were on board, the senior ships' officers and the expedition team would dine in the big passenger restaurant on deck four, but the rest mostly stayed below decks, in the crew areas.

These past two days had been one of the steepest learning curves of Jenny's life. With no passengers to worry about yet, the ship and its crew were being tested. They'd had lifeboat drill. Fire drill. Impact drill. Bomb drill. That one had seemed very strange to Jenny. Who would want to bomb a cruise ship in the middle of the ocean? Jenny had learned how to check a waterproof door, use a fire extinguisher, communicate with the bridge and now, don a life jacket. In between drills, she'd been given her lecture schedule and was learning the rules of passenger management.

The passengers, of course, were in a totally different class to all the crew. In more ways than one. They were the customers — not always right — but to be treated as if they were. This cruise was apparently the very latest in luxury adventure holidays . . . which meant the passengers would be rich and probably used to getting their own way.

It had all been totally foreign and totally exhausting, yet she'd still managed to find the energy every night to go up to deck eight. She told herself it was to look at the stars, and enjoy the fresh air while it was still warm. It wasn't in the hope of seeing the mysterious passenger from the sauna — and it most definitely was not in the hope of seeing him *in* the sauna.

Jenny had met all of the expedition crew during the past few days, and quite a few of the hotel staff. As casually as she could, she'd mentioned the mysterious passenger in cabin 642. No one knew who he was. Speculation was rife as to his identity — and why he was on board. Some thought he was spying for their cruise line owners — looking for people to sack. Others thought he was some sort of security expert following up on a threat to the ship. That rumour had a sudden surge in popularity during the bomb drill. One small group thought he was some millionaire planning to buy the ship for his private use. The fact was — no one really knew. No one had even seen him, except the stewards who had taken meals to his cabin. Room service was not normally offered on board the *Cape Adare*, yet another mark of his VIP status. No one had seen him outside his cabin. No one that was, except Jenny, and she kept that incident to herself.

She was desperate to see him again. Well, no. Not desperate — that sounded awful. But she was intrigued. Who wouldn't be?

'That's you done then,' Karl's voice reminded Jenny that she was in the middle of lifeboat training.

'Sorry?'

'That's it. Finished. You passed. The lives of our passengers are now officially safe in your hands.'

'God help them,' Jenny muttered, but Karl just smiled.

'You'll do just fine. We dock in

Hobart at 0600 tomorrow for passengers and supplies. You can go ashore between eight and twelve if you want. Any last minute shopping. That sort of thing.'

'Great. Thanks.'

'It's going to get busy after that. We've got a full day and two nights at sea before our first excursion. That's a lot of time to keep the passengers occupied. Are you ready for your first lecture?'

'I think so. I'm going to work on it some more tonight.'

* * *

The ship's library was on deck four — along with the lecture theatre, restaurant and one of the ship's two bars. Jenny headed there immediately after dinner. The rest of the crew were crowded into the recreation spaces downstairs, making the most of their last night without passengers. Jenny was nervous about her on-board lectures, which was strange given that she had been teaching at university for the past two years. But that had been different. They were students. The passengers were . . . well . . . real people. People who had paid a lot of money for their cruise. She didn't want to let them down. And she didn't want to let Karl down either. The big Norwegian and his wife had been kind to her since her arrival. She was now fully equipped with uniforms — practical black slacks and crisp white shirts. As well as this, she had several heavy jumpers, thick socks and gum boots, a waterproof jacket, fur lined gloves (artificial fur of course) and a new rucksack stashed in her cabin. Everything a fashion conscious girl needed to walk into a freezer.

Jenny paused outside the library door, her eyes drifting towards the stairwell that led to deck eight and the sauna. No. Not tonight. Stalker was such an ugly word. Tonight she'd just work on her lectures.

The library was empty and quiet.

Jenny opened her laptop and set to work. Karl had given her some material prepared by the lecturer whose place she had taken. There were notes and slides and handouts. All Jenny really needed to do was familiarise herself with them — and make sure she was ready to answer any questions her audience had. Luckily the library was full of books about Antarctica, and she piled several of them on the table next to her computer.

After working for about an hour, she ducked outside to the bathroom. As she was returning, she noticed someone behind the bar. The lights were on and for the first time since boarding the ship, Jenny decided she could use a drink.

'Hi,' she said to the girl behind the bar. 'Are you open? Can I get a drink?'

'We're not officially open, but I guess I can manage something,' the girl replied with a smile. 'What do you want? Juice? Coke?'

'Either is fine — as long as there is

some vodka in it,' Jenny replied.

The girl behind the bar laughed, and then frowned. 'You're joking, right?'

'No, why would I be joking?' Jenny asked.

'Because the crew aren't allowed to drink . . . ' the girl answered, as if explaining something to a child.

'I know we can't drink if we are on duty. But there aren't even any passengers on board.'

'We are not allowed to drink on board. Ever. Passengers or not.'

Jenny let that sink in.

'You mean, I can't even have a glass of wine until we get back in . . . twenty days or something?'

'That's right.'

Jenny blinked a couple of times. 'But that's . . . '

The girl behind the bar looked at her with raised eyebrows. 'You've been on board for two days now. Hadn't you noticed there was no booze in the crew mess?'

She had, but she hadn't really given it

much thought. She'd had too many other things on her mind. Now that she did think about it she could see the logic. She wondered why Mr Schofield hadn't said something during her interview back in Sydney. Come to think of it, he probably had. She really hadn't been listening all that well.

'Can I have a Coke, please?'

'Sure. On the house,' the girl pulled a can from the fridge.

'Thanks.'

Jenny hurried back towards the library. She could feel the girl's eyes following her. She must think she had a drinking problem or something. Which she didn't. She just liked a glass of wine with her meals. And maybe something a bit stronger after a tough day — and by all appearances, she had plenty of those ahead of her. Of course, she could always jump ship when they docked in Hobart next day. She smiled. Two days ago, she might have given that some serious thought, but now she was beginning to enjoy herself. The crew were friendly, if not yet friends. She was busy enough that it was easy to keep thoughts of Ray at bay — well, almost easy. There had been a few moments, lying alone in her cabin . . . But her busy days helped. Then there was the mysterious passenger in cabin 642 . . .

Jenny reached for the library door. As she did, the can of Coke slipped from her fingers. It landed on the carpet with a dull thud, and rolled away. Jenny made a wild grab for it, and took it with her back into the library. She put the can down on the table, eyeing it suspiciously. She wasn't about to open it now. She'd made that mistake before.

She resumed her seat, opened her laptop and set to work again, a notebook close by her hand. She had just about completed her notes when a voice spoke very close to her ear.

'Would you mind — that's really quite annoying.'

Jenny jumped to her feet, dropping the pen she had been holding. 'What?'

The mysterious man from the sauna

bent over to retrieve the pen. His strong fingers curled around it, then depressed the end. Click. He did it again. Click. And again. Click. Click.

'I'm sorry,' Jenny said, realisation coming to her. 'I do that when I'm working.'

'Maybe you should get a pen that doesn't click,' the man said.

'Ah, yes. I will.'

Up close and clothed, he was equally as gorgeous as he'd been in the sauna. His eyes, she was surprised to discover, were blue. A darker blue than any she had seen before. With his fair skin and dark hair, it was quite a startling face. Startling and compelling. He obviously hadn't shaved for a day or two. The stubble on his jaw was as dark as his hair. He was wearing a polo shirt, the open neck giving just a tantalising glimpse of dark hair on his chest. She remembered how that chest had looked in the sauna, glistening with sweat that trickled down his skin towards . . .

'Your pen?' He was holding it out to

her. His voice was a perfect match for his perfect face and body. Dark and rich . . . not Darth Vader so much as dark chocolate.

'Ah. Yes. Thanks.' She took it, being very careful that her fingers didn't touch his as she did. If their fingers touched, she would be electrocuted. She was sure of it.

'Goodnight.' He headed for the door.

Jenny watched him move. He had great shoulders, legs that went on forever and the best bum she had seen in a long time. He paused by the door, and turned back towards her, his lips twitching in a smile. He knew she'd been watching him!

Flustered, Jenny dropped back into her chair, and busied herself opening her can of drink. She pulled the ring tab on the can and it exploded, spraying foamy cold liquid across the table.

'Crap!' Jenny directed the spray away from her precious laptop. The dark foam splattered across the back of a chair.

Mortified, Jenny darted across to a metal waste bin, using it to catch the last of the drink dripping from the can. Her hands were covered in sweet sticky liquid. The dark stains on her clothes were from the same source. The can in her hand was now considerably lighter, and still dripping.

'Damn it!' With a sigh of exasperation, she let the can fall, gently, into the waste bin. Now it was someone else's problem. Too embarrassed to look up, she stared down at the table, to see a few drops of thick dark liquid trickling down the screen of her laptop. And the book next to it was starting to crinkle.

'Shit and double shit!' Jenny pulled her white uniform shirt out of her slacks and used the tail to wipe the computer screen. Then she dabbed at the book.

'Try this.' Her companion had returned to her side. He held out his handkerchief.

'Thanks.' Jenny patted the book a bit more. It was a large hardback, full of spectacular colour photographs of Antarctica. On the open page, a penguin's face was starting to appear rather soggy. 'He looks a bit sad now, doesn't he?'

The man beside her chuckled. The sound sent a pleasant tingle up her spine. 'I've never seen a cheerful penguin.'

This time, Jenny laughed. She turned away from the book and looked back up into the blue eyes. 'I truly am sorry. About the swearing. If you want to complain to the captain, my name is Jenny Payne. I'm an expedition specialist.'

'Pleased to meet you, Jenny Payne, expedition specialist.' He held out his hand.

Jenny placed her hand in his. Instead of the shock she had expected, the hand that closed around hers seemed almost cold. Strong . . . but there was no warmth in it.

'I'm pretty sure the captain doesn't need to know about this.' He detached his hand from hers. 'Goodnight.'

'Goodnight.'

Jenny watched him walk away. It wasn't until after the door had closed behind him that she realised he had not told her his name. She let her gaze fall to the handkerchief on the table, next to the Coke-stained book.

'Who is that man?' she asked, but the sad, soggy penguin did not reply.

5

'What a nice looking ship,' Vera Horsley said as she approached the big vessel tied up next to the dock. 'Don't you think so, my dear?'

Her daughter walking next to her didn't look too enthused. 'Are you sure you want to do this Mum?'

'Of course I'm sure. Why shouldn't I want to do this?'

'Antarctica seems such a long way. And you'll be missing Christmas dinner with the family. Maybe you should wait until someone can come with you. When the kids are back at college, I could . . . '

'Nonsense, Mary. I'll be fine by myself. Just because I'm not as young as I was, there's no call for you to start thinking I'm in my dotage. Seventy is not old.'

'No, Mum.'

Everything about Mary's voice suggested that she actually thought seventy-year-old mothers should be whiling away their days knitting shawls, and not setting out on expeditions to the South Pole. Vera chose to ignore her.

'I am sorry about Christmas,' she added in a conciliatory tone. 'But this was the only cruise available. And Christmas in Antarctica does sound like fun.'

Mary gave a derisive snort.

'If you could just help me with my bag,' Vera said, 'you don't have to wait around until the ship sails. I shall be perfectly all right on my own.' Vera did not add that she'd prefer to explore the ship alone, without her daughter's disapproval to spoil her fun.

A large section of the massive steel hull appeared to have been folded up, creating an opening in the ship's side. A long, gently sloping ramp led to a set of stairs which would take her into the brightly-lit interior. Vera settled her large purple bag more comfortably on her arm and took a firm grip on the railing. Despite her brave words to her daughter, her not-quite-as-young-as-it-used-to-be body did sometimes let her down, and she wasn't going to risk a fall now. Nothing was going to keep her from being on board this ship as it sailed out of the Derwent River estuary, leaving Hobart in its wake.

'Welcome aboard the *Cape Adare*.' A young man in uniform was standing at the top of the ramp.

'Thank you.' Vera felt just the tiniest thrill as she stepped over the threshold.

'If you go through there, the receptionist will help you.'

Vera followed his instructions, and made her way to a lovely polished wooden desk. 'This is just like checking in to a hotel,' she told the girl behind the desk.

'Yes, Ma'am. That's exactly what it's like. And here is your room key.' The girl presented her with a piece of hard plastic about the size of a credit card.

'This also allows us to keep a record of who enters and leaves the ship,' the girl added. 'So you will have to present it whenever you set out on an excursion. And when you come back. That way we can be sure you don't get left behind.' The girl grinned.

'I'm not so sure about those excursions, Mother,' Mary said as they set out in search of Vera's cabin. 'Reading the brochure, they sounded a bit much for you. Open boats. Walking on the ice. You need to be careful.'

'I will be,' Vera said, thinking all the while that the excursions sounded rather fun.

'Now, Mother, you are on deck five. The Shackleton Suite. Cabin number 543. The lifts are just over here.'

Vera looked about with interest as they made their way to her cabin. The ship was more luxurious than she had thought it would be. The blue carpets were thick and soft. The pastel shaded walls adorned with rather lovely framed photographs of ships and icebergs and assorted wild things. She was starting to feel very excited.

'Here you are, Mum. This door looks like it's made of iron. Isn't that going to be difficult for you to manage?'

'Not at all.' Vera gritted her teeth, trying to appear at ease as she swung the heavy door open.

Mary followed her in to the cabin, and deposited her bag on the bed. 'It's supposed to be a suite. This doesn't look like a suite. It's awfully small. I should go back and talk to that girl at reception. She must have made a mistake.'

'Don't be silly,' Vera said sharply. 'It said the name of the suite on the door. This is the right cabin. It's more than enough room for me, and look, there's a balcony.'

'Won't that be a bit cold when you get right down . . . there?'

Vera suppressed a sigh. Mary wasn't that bad. Not really. She was just a terrible fusspot who worried about anything and everything. She'd worry if she had nothing to worry about. In moments of absolute honesty, Vera knew she was partly to blame for that. Mary had always been of a nervous disposition, and it can't have been easy for her, as a child, to overhear all those conversations about grisly crimes and murder trials. She was making this much fuss because she loved her mother, and didn't want her going to such a wild and distant place on her own. Although Vera understood all that, and loved her daughter dearly, it was hard to take sometimes.

'I'm sure it will be just lovely. After all, it is summer.'

'Yes, but I read that the temperature never gets above freezing down there — even in summer.'

'I'm well prepared.' Vera opened her suitcase, the woolly contents of which immediately overflowed onto the bed. 'You've made sure I have everything I need.'

'Well . . . '

'I'm fine. Honestly. Why don't you

head off now? I'll just unpack. Look, there's a kettle. I can make a nice cup of tea and then later on I shall go on deck as we sail.'

'All right then, Mother. If you're absolutely certain . . . ?'

'I am.' Vera felt an unexpected wave of affection as she hugged her daughter goodbye. 'Don't worry about me. I'll be fine.'

'You call me. Or get one of the staff to help you e-mail, if they have it. Just so I know you are all right.'

Vera nodded. Mary had never quite grasped the fact that her short, elderly, grey-haired mother probably spent more time in front of a computer than she did. The sound of the door closing brought a wave of welcome relief to Vera. She made no attempt to unpack. Or to make a cup of tea. She found the ship's information brochure on the desk and studied the plan. The passenger observation lounge looked good. It had a bar. Vera wondered if it was too early in the day for a G&T. Surely not. Not when she was about to begin the adventure of a lifetime. A small cocktail wouldn't hurt. She opened the door and looked down the hallway. Mary had long since vanished. Slipping her room key into her voluminous handbag next to her notebook and pen, Vera set off in search of adventure.

*   *   *

Lian Chang put her bag down on her bunk and looked around. The cabin was tiny. Even smaller than she had expected. Cabin 320 was an inside cabin, which meant no porthole. No daylight. It was well lit but just a bit claustrophobic. Still, it had been the cheapest cabin she could get. This trip was all about timing and money.

It didn't take her long to unpack. Her case held mostly jeans and jumpers. She grimaced slightly as she put the jeans away. She wouldn't grow out of them in just three weeks. Would she? She laid her hand across her stomach. No bump. Not yet. She wasn't sure when it would start to show. Hopefully not too soon. Not before she got to the ice. To Colin. His photograph was in the bottom of her bag. She sat down on the bed and stared at his face. Colin had such beautiful blue eyes and a shock of sun bleached blond hair. By comparison, her hair was long and dark and straight, her eyes so brown they were almost black against the golden tones of her skin. Everyone said they made such an attractive couple. Everyone except her parents. They'd never met Colin. They would be horrified to think of their daughter with a *gweilo*. A ghost. A foreigner.

And now . . .

She put her hand on her stomach again. For her conservative parents, marriage to anyone other than the son of a good Chinese family was out of the question. And if they knew . . .

But they didn't. At least, not yet. They didn't know she was on board this ship. They thought she was up in Queensland, visiting the Gold Coast with her girlfriends. By the time they found out she wasn't there, it would be too late. She would be on her way to find Colin. She would tell him about the baby and they would announce they were engaged. Would her parents accept a white son-in-law and a mixed race grandchild?

'They have to,' she whispered. 'But it doesn't matter if they don't. We'll love our baby.'

Of course they would. Even though the baby was an accident, Colin would love it. She was certain of that.

Almost certain.

Lian got to her feet. Sitting here moping was doing her no good at all. The ship was due to sail in a little while. Maybe she should go up on deck to watch. It wasn't as if her parents were about to appear and drag her off the boat. And if they tried — well, she was twenty-one years old. That was old enough to make her own decisions! Not even her parents could override the law in their adopted country.

As she set off down the passage towards the lifts, Lian spotted a crowd of people in the entrance area. More passengers arriving, she guessed. The third deck was the poor end of the passenger accommodation, but it was also the lobby and reception desk. Once they were away from port, she guessed — she hoped — that most of the passengers would remain on the upper decks. She was looking for a little peace and quiet.

'Sorry.' A tall gangly youth with a huge rucksack tried to push past her. For a few seconds they did a tiny dance in the hallway.

'Hey! Barstow! What are you doing to that poor girl?' Another youth appeared. This one was shorter, but solidly built. 'Hello there!' he beamed at Lian. 'Is this chap bothering you?' Lian wasn't sure if the upper crust English accent was real or just put on.

'No. Really. I was just heading to the lifts.'

'Are you down here with us?'

With the arrival of the third youth, Lian suddenly realised that they all had something in common. Each was wearing a sweatshirt emblazoned with some sort of crest. She looked more closely at their faces. Seventeen, she guessed. Maybe eighteen.

'I say, Barstow, she's far too lovely for you.' The newcomer angled his body between Lian and the tall youth. 'She's obviously a girl of taste and discernment, so you're out too Miles. I am, on the other hand, just . . . '

'Gentlemen. I hope you're not bothering that young lady!'

'No, sir.' The three youths almost snapped to attention as an older man approached.

'All right, why don't you go and find your cabins. Then round up the rest of them. Let's meet in the lounge on deck five in fifteen minutes. I want to do a head count as we depart — just to make sure no one has fallen overboard before we even leave port.'

'OK.' With an assortment of grins and winks, the three youths vanished down the corridor. Lian could hear them laughing as they went.

'I hope they didn't upset you,' the older man said courteously.

'No. It's fine, really,' Lian assured him. 'Are you all really English?'

'Yes. It's gap year for them . . . They are taking a year off between school and university,' he explained when he saw Lian's frown. 'I'm their teacher. I'm also supposed to be the chaperone.'

'Good luck.'

'I might just need it.' A sudden yell echoed from further down the corridor. 'They are harmless really. Well, mostly harmless and they will settle down. But if you do have any problems, don't hesitate to come and find me.'

'I'm sure they'll be fine. Thanks.'

Lian resumed her journey. A group of hormone-fuelled teenagers wasn't her first choice for travelling companions, but it didn't really bother her. They might be a bit noisy, but perhaps having some cheerful voices and all that youthful exuberance nearby would take her mind off things once in a while.

The lift had just deposited another two passengers when Lian arrived in the lobby. She quickly jumped aboard and pressed the button for deck seven. She guessed she'd get all the fresh air she needed up there.

At deck five, the lift paused and the doors slid open. An elderly woman clutching a huge purple handbag smiled at Lian as she joined her. A few seconds later, they had reached deck eight.

'Thank you,' the elderly woman said as Lian stood back to let her alight from the lift. Lian followed her, a little surprised to see someone of her age on board the ship. Still, she thought, she was hardly the right person to question anyone's motives for making this journey.

★ ★ ★

A huge crowd of people had gathered at the dock to wave farewell to the *Cape Adare*. The first sailing of a new, luxurious cruise ship to the most remote place on Earth was news. From her vantage point on the eighth deck, Jenny saw a sea of faces smiling up at her. People below were waving at friends and relatives on board the ship, while the hinged section of the great steel hull slowly folded back into place, sealing the gangway entrance against the ocean. Uniformed men scuttled around the dock, releasing the huge ropes that had held the ship fast. All it needed now was a brass band to give it a real sense of occasion.

She could hear the ship's engine, a low background noise, but at first there was no real sensation of movement. A thin gap appeared between the ship's hull and the dock, gradually growing wider. Then the ship began to move slowly forward. It had docked facing up the river, looking towards the graceful arc of the Tasman Bridge that spanned the estuary. Now, slowly, the *Cape Adare* began to turn, pointing her eager bow to the south.

The crowd on the dock was beginning to disperse, but not so the crowd on the observation deck. Jenny could see bright smiling faces all around her, people eager for adventure. They were a mixed group, of all ages, although no children were allowed on the cruise. She'd heard quite a few English accents, particularly among the lads leaning precariously over the side railing. There were quite a lot of couples, holding hands and smiling at each other in anticipation of the adventure ahead. Jenny sighed as she looked at them. If only . . . she thrust that thought aside. This wasn't a time for self-pity. She had an adventure ahead — and who knew what was in store for her. She let her eyes wander once more over the excited and happy crowd.

The face she was looking for wasn't there. The man from cabin 642 obviously had no one to wave goodbye to him from Hobart dock. She wondered if there had been anyone at Sydney to wave him away on his journey — or had he also spent that departure alone in the confines of his cabin?

6

'I'd like to welcome you all on board the *Cape Adare*, for this expedition to the last great wilderness on the planet.'

Captain Haugen's words drew a smattering of cheers from the people gathered in the observation lounge.

'During the next twenty days, you will see the place described by Captain James Cook as a country doomed never to feel the warmth of the sun — but to lie forever buried under snow and ice. Cook felt that any man — or woman — who ventured there was quite welcome to the experience. But fear not — for there were other early explorers who felt the Antarctic was full of wonders beyond our powers to imagine. And I, for one, agree with them.'

Jenny looked around the crowded lounge, but she didn't see the face she was looking for. Her tall, dark and handsome 'friend' was probably the only passenger not present for the captain's pre-dinner welcome. The passengers were there for the free cocktails, and to find out what lay ahead of them. Jenny, like the rest of the expedition team, was there because it was part of her job. And, like the other crew members, she would be toasting the success of the voyage in soda rather than champagne. Despite that, she was rather enjoying herself. In some ways, she was finding it surprisingly liberating to be among total strangers. No one here had any expectations of her, apart from doing the job she was being paid to do.

The captain had finished his speech, and now it was Karl's turn to outline the programme for the expedition, and the rules. Most of it was familiar to Jenny. She'd been reading up on such things during the past day and a half at sea, when not fighting with a life jacket or exploding Coke cans in front of handsome men. She looked around the room again, as Karl announced a full lifeboat drill for the next morning.

'No one is excused,' the expedition leader said loudly. 'This is a safety requirement under maritime law. The good news is that despite the many, many times my crew has run this drill, we've never had to use it for real . . . yet.'

The listening passengers laughed on cue. So did Karl's team who had no doubt heard the line before.

'After the drill, the first seminar of the voyage will take place in the Wilkes Lecture Theatre on Deck Four. You'll be hearing from Jenny Payne — who'll be talking about our first destination — Macquarie Island. We'll reach the island early the next morning — so you want to be prepared.'

Jenny felt a few eyes turn her way. She smiled and nodded confidently.

'Each evening, the next day's schedule will be available from the expedition desk which is also on deck four, and conveniently close to the bar.' That gave rise to another round of laughter, but the passengers were getting restless. It was time for that pre-dinner cocktail.

As if sensing the moment, Karl finished his speech by inviting all the passengers to the bar for a complementary drink. Jenny stepped aside in case she was trampled in the rush. As she did, she kept her eyes open for a shock of dark hair.

'He isn't here then, dear?'

'Sorry?' Startled, Jenny looked down at the speaker. The woman had to be seventy if she was a day. She was short, and almost as round as she was tall. Her eyes were a much darker grey than her hair, and they twinkled as she spoke. She was clutching an enormous purple handbag.

'You were obviously looking for someone. I assume anyone who could cause that much interest in a young girl like yourself must be a man.'

'I . . . I was just wondering who I might have on my table for dinner,' Jenny replied, clutching at straws. Each of the expedition team was assigned a table for lunch and dinner, where they were expected to chat to the passengers. It was just part of the job. Jenny was starting to realise there would be no 'days off' during the next three weeks, and very little personal time. That wasn't such a bad thing, though. If she was busy, she wouldn't be worrying about what the hell she was going to do when she made it back to dry land again, or thinking about Ray . . . or . . .

'Of course you were,' the elderly lady continued in a conspiratorial tone. 'Tell me, is he frightfully handsome?'

Jenny started to smile. There was something in the woman's face that made it hard to do otherwise. 'I'm not telling you anything about him,' Jenny said with mock severity. 'You'd probably steal him away from under my nose.'

'In my youth, I might have done just that,' the older woman replied. 'But I'm afraid my stealing days are over.'

They both laughed.

'You're Jenny — our lecturer tomorrow, aren't you?' the woman asked.

'That's right.'

'It's nice to meet you, Jenny. I'm Vera Horsley.'

Something about the name seemed vaguely familiar to Jenny, but looking down at the woman, she knew they'd never met before. 'Welcome on board, Mrs Horsley.'

'Please call me Vera. Do you have some gruesome tales for us? Shipwrecks? Cannibals perhaps? There's nothing like a bit of death and disaster to set the pulse racing.'

'You'll just have to wait and see,' Jenny said.

'I'll be in the front row,' Vera promised. 'Now, Jenny is that the ship's doctor I spy over there. That charming gentleman with all the gold braid?'

Jenny followed Vera's nod. 'Yes, that's him. Are you feeling unwell? I'll go and get him . . . '

'No. Don't worry. I'm fine. I just want to have a little chat with him

117

about amputating frostbitten toes.'

Of course you do, Jenny thought as Vera and her purple handbag set off across the room. What a strange woman. Nice — but strange. Jenny wasn't at all sure if she wanted Vera on her table at dinner, or not. Conversations about surgical procedures were not exactly the sort of table talk she was looking for.

She need not have worried. By accident or possibly design, Vera was seated with the ship's doctor just two tables from Jenny's seat near the glass doors leading to a small balcony at the rear of the restaurant. Until now, Jenny had taken all her meals in the crew mess, and it was nice to enjoy the more luxurious surroundings. Her dinner companions included an English teacher, who was apparently chaperoning a group of youths on a school related adventure. The teenagers in question were seated at two nearby tables, for which Jenny was secretly glad. She hadn't escaped her university students just to take on another group. The chaperone, Eric Dempsey looked to be about thirty. He seemed a nice man, very polite. He already knew the tiny Asian girl who was seated with them. The girl, Lian Chang, was extremely pretty, but very quiet. The food was very good, but Lian didn't eat much. She pushed the food around her plate and sent it back almost untouched.

'If the food isn't to your liking,' Jenny offered, 'I'm sure we can arrange something else.'

'No. That's not it at all. I'm just feeling a bit queasy. Seasick, no doubt.'

Jenny hoped for Lian's sake she wasn't seasick. The weather at the moment was good — the water quite calm. According to Karl, once they hit the southern ocean, things would be entirely different, and Jenny had already equipped herself with a generous supply of seasickness pills. The meal passed pleasantly enough, although Lian excused herself immediately after not eating her dessert. Jenny was wondering if she should offer to help the girl, when she became aware of a crowd developing around her table.

'Gentlemen, this is Miss Payne. She's a lecturer on the expedition team,' Eric explained to the gathering of young men.

'Wow. The lecturers back home don't look like you,' one of the youths commented.

'Enough of that,' Eric said sternly.

'Sorry.' The young man looked contrite.

Jenny smiled to show that everything was fine. She'd dealt with more than a few over-exuberant school leavers in her day. These English boys couldn't be any worse than the West Sydney lads, although for some reason their accents and manners made them seem older than they were. The thought did occur to her that she should have a quiet word with the hotel manager. The bar staff might need to be on the alert.

One of the things that Vera had noticed about getting old was the fact that she didn't sleep as much as she once had. These days, waking up at five o'clock in the morning usually meant a cup of tea in bed with a good book. Not this morning though. This morning she stepped smartly out of bed and dressed quickly. Taking her cup of tea, she set out towards the observation lounge. It was just getting light outside. She thought it might be fun to watch the sun rise, while she waited for the rest of the ship to come alive.

As she stood in the glass sided lift, slowly ascending to deck seven, Vera saw some feet on the stairs. As she went up, the feet came down, and their owner glanced at her briefly as she sailed silently past. My, she thought. He was handsome. No wonder that young lecturer was interested. Any woman who wasn't interested in a man who looked like that was probably dead.

When the lift deposited her outside the observation lounge, Vera moved quickly to the stairs and looked down. The stairs were empty. He must have stopped at deck six. Probably a passenger heading back to his cabin. Strange though that he should be up and about this early. Normally it was only old folk like her who couldn't sleep.

Shrugging, Vera walked through into the observation lounge. It was empty, as she suspected. She moved towards the huge glass windows that overlooked the bow of the ship, and the seemingly endless ocean beyond. In the dim pre-dawn light, the water looked dark and forbidding. Vera tried to imagine being alone out here in a small boat. Maybe adrift. Or lost. She shivered. *Hic sunt dracones*! Here there be dragons!

She lowered her handbag onto a chair, and was about to sit down, when she noticed something lying on an adjoining table. It was a paper napkin, but there was something drawn on it.

Vera fetched it, and sat down to study it.

Someone had drawn a man's hand on the napkin. Despite the flimsy nature of the paper, the hand itself evoked great strength. The fingers were long and powerful. They could have gripped a gun, or a woman, with equal ease. Vera's eyes were drawn to the ring on the middle finger. A skull ring. It didn't look like the sort of ring that would go with a motorcycle jacket and tattoos. The ring appeared finely crafted. A ring with a message that went beyond mere masculine posturing.

'This is very good,' Vera murmured to herself. 'I wonder . . . '

She looked around the room, but there was no one else there. It might have been left behind by the man she'd seen earlier. Vera settled herself comfortably in her chair and placed the napkin on the table in front of her. Smiling, she reached into her bag and pulled out her ever-present notebook and pen.

When she set out for breakfast an hour and a half later, Vera took the napkin with her, folded carefully inside the cover of her notebook.

Breakfast was a far less formal affair than dinner, and this early, there weren't many people about, so passengers could sit wherever they fancied. Vera looked about hopefully for the doctor. She had some questions for him about how long a person could survive in the icy waters around Antarctica. Not long, she imagined, but she wanted to make sure she got it right. There was no sign of the doctor, but she did notice another familiar face.

'Good morning, Jenny. How are you?'

'Hello, Mrs . . . Vera. I'm fine, thank you. You're up early.'

'One of the things about growing old. When you haven't got many years left, you don't want to waste them sleeping.'

'Something tells me you were never one for wasting time.'

Vera laughed as she went to collect

her breakfast from the selection laid out on the buffet. When she returned to the table, she asked Jenny about lifeboat drill.

'I've never been on a cruise before, you see,' she said. 'I want to make sure I understand everything.'

'Shall I tell you a secret?' Jenny whispered. 'This is my first cruise too.'

'How wonderful,' Vera was delighted. 'We can explore this together then. Which is your lifeboat?'

'Starboard side.'

'That's left. Right?'

'No, Vera, it's the right side.'

'I think I should write that down.' Vera pulled out her notebook. 'Port is the left. Starboard on the right. Now, if I was the sort of person who would forget that, how would I be able to remember?'

'Well,' Jenny explained, 'there are a couple of ways. For example, left is the shorter word — and so is port.'

That was good. Vera wrote it down.

Vera stayed in the restaurant, even

after Jenny left. She loved sitting quietly and watching people. She chuckled as she watched the English lads flirting with the waitresses as they cleared the tables. A couple of ships' officers appeared briefly. Vera looked closely at their uniforms, and then consulted her notes. One had a small golden propeller embroidered on his sleeve. An engineer. The other, with the gold diamond on his sleeve was bridge crew. Navigation officer, she guessed.

A sudden flurry of activity dragged her attention to a nearby table. The group of English lads was trying to get the attention of the pretty Asian girl she'd met briefly last night. It was obvious they wanted her to join their group at a large table near the window, but it was also just as obvious that she wasn't too keen. She was standing near the buffet table, holding a tray and looking just a little lost. Vera waved to catch her eye, then smiled and gestured to her to join her table.

'May I sit here?' the girl asked a little

shyly as she approached.

'Of course,' Vera said. She glanced over at the schoolboys. 'They are just a little bit too much on an empty stomach, aren't they?'

'Oh . . . they aren't too bad. It's just that I'm on their deck, and I really don't want to encourage them. And anyway, I'm . . . ' The girl's voice tapered off.

'Yes?' Vera wasn't one to pry — well, if she was perfectly honest with herself, she was. People were fascinating, and she loved finding out all about everyone she met. But in a nice way . . .

'I'm on my way to meet my boyfriend — well, fiancé. He works at one of the Antarctic research stations.'

Now that really was interesting. 'You must tell me all about it, my dear. By the way, my name is Vera. Vera Horsley.'

'I'm Lian Chang.'

They were still chatting when the ship's horn gave a series of short sharp blasts.

'That will be the lifeboat drill,' Vera

said. 'How very exciting. Shall we go together Lian?'

They made their way from the restaurant towards the stairs. A crew member appeared next to them, already wearing his orange life jacket. He directed them to the nearest lifeboat, which was up one level on deck five. Vera watched with interest as the crew gave instructions on how to don a life jacket. She was busy taking notes, when a crewman approached her.

'I'm sorry, Ma'am. You've got to put the jacket on now. Please.'

'Oh, yes of course.' Vera carefully placed her notebook back in her bag, which she placed with equal care at her feet. With Lian's help, she donned the cumbersome orange affair. It felt slightly uncomfortable, and not surprisingly, smelled of rubber. She bent to retrieve her notebook and add that detail.

All through the drill, Vera kept her eyes peeled for the handsome man she had seen earlier that morning. He didn't appear. She didn't see Jenny Payne either. Perhaps they were both on the other side of the ship, where the second lifeboat hung in its gantry. She would ask in a little while, when she saw Jenny at the lecture theatre. The Wilkes theatre, it was called. As they were thanked for their time and told they could go, Vera wondered if Jenny knew that the theatre had been named after the seaman who was said to have inspired Herman Melville's mad Captain Ahab in *Moby Dick*. Vera made a mental note to tell her.

7

'In the 1800s, Macquarie Island was considered too remote, too wild and inhospitable even to be a penal colony,' Jenny said, 'so it may surprise you to learn there are now well over four million inhabitants there ... ' She paused as a baffled murmur ran through her audience. 'Of course, most of them are penguins.'

She was rewarded with a round of laughter.

Jenny felt a familiar glow of contentment as she looked around the room. The faces there were generally much older than the students in her classrooms back in Sydney, but what mattered was the light in those faces. They were interested in what she was saying. They were learning, and the things that she was teaching them were helping to build an understanding and appreciation of the world around them. This was exactly what she had always wanted from teaching. She was surprised to find such satisfaction in a job she had taken purely from desperation.

'Four million penguins is a lot of penguin poo,' Jenny continued, 'so when you go ashore, make sure you've got your gumboots on.'

That got another ripple of laughter.

'For the English among us,' Jenny added as she noticed the frowns on several young male faces, 'gumboots are Wellington boots with Aussie accents.'

Jenny guessed that almost every passenger from the ship was sitting in the lecture hall. She recognised Vera Horsley and Lian sitting together in the front row. Vera's notebook was being put to good use. The English lads and their teacher were a bit further back. As was Karl. The expedition leader smiled and nodded as she caught his eye. She must be doing all right. The one face that wasn't there was the one she had most hoped to see. Obviously their encounter in the library had not been enough to entice the passenger from cabin 642 to her lecture.

'Excuse me, Jenny. Can you tell us about the shipwrecks?'

'Of course, I can, Vera.' Who else would have asked that question? 'And for those of you who think shipwrecks only happened in times of yore — let me tell you that the last ship to run aground where we are heading was in 1987. Would you believe, it was the ship belonging to the Australian Antarctic Research Expedition — let's hope we do a bit better than they did.'

After the lecture, Jenny stayed back in the theatre, chatting to a few people about the things they would see when they reached the island. Eventually, they all left, heading for the restaurant where a seafood buffet lunch was about to be served. Jenny finished tidying up, then left. Outside the theatre, she stopped at the internet station. The ship's satellite links gave e-mail access to her wealthy passengers even in the middle of the ocean. Jenny was supposed to use the staff stations in the crew quarters. She'd done that already to e-mail her family and assure them she was fine and having fun. Right now, everyone was at lunch, it would only take a minute to check for new mail . . . because she knew what she would find.

Nothing.

Ray still hadn't tried to get in touch. No phone call. No text. No e-mail. There were a few e-mails from her former colleagues, asking about her sudden disappearance. Some even mentioned Ray's sudden engagement. She wasn't in the mood to answer them or to talk about Ray. But she did answer the e-mails from her family, assuring them she was fine and enjoying her cruise. She felt guilty about allowing them to think she was on holiday. There was also the matter of Christmas and her absence from the family dinner to mention. But not today.

Jenny logged out of her account and headed up the stairs to deck seven. She wasn't really in the mood for lunch and after an hour and a half of talking, she needed a little peace and quiet. Time to herself. She emerged on the deck, taking long deep draughts of the fresh crisp air. The ship had come a long way south since she boarded, and it was noticeably cooler. Jenny made her way towards the back of the ship, and leaned against the side rail in the relative shelter of the ship's funnel. She watched the water streaming past. The sea here was a deeper shade of grey blue than the warmer waters she was used to. The waves splashed and foamed at the ship's side. The ocean so far had been calm, but Jenny knew there were stormy waters ahead, when the ship reached the southern ocean. She had shown no signs of seasickness yet . . . and with luck she would escape that particular unpleasantness. She appeared to have found her sea legs quite easily.

This running away was easier than she had thought. Because that's what she was doing. Running away from Ray, and the pain he'd caused her. Running away from the image of his pregnant fiancée and her own self-disgust. That last bit wasn't proving too easy. It wasn't that she was hoping for some sort of reconciliation. She wasn't. All she wanted was some small sign that Ray missed her. That her leaving had caused him some distress. Even a tiny twinge of remorse? Would an e-mail or a text have cost him so much? Did he even realise she was gone? And maybe he was pleased that she was.

Jenny sighed.

She leaned even further forward to look down into the water. Why couldn't she have a *Titanic* moment? Some Leonardo DiCaprio lookalike should come dashing forward about now to save her from jumping into the ocean in a fit of despair. Not that she would jump, of course. The water looked far too cold . . . but it would be nice to think someone would rescue her if she tried . . .

Suddenly, a face emerged from the waves, dark eyes smiling up at her. A large black and white body curved free of the waves, arched and then plunged back in to disappear as quickly as it had come.

A dolphin? Here. They were a bit far south for dolphins . . . unless . . .

She leaned ever further over the rail, her eyes searching the water. She was rewarded a few seconds later as another dolphin broke the water, leaping upwards, water droplets surrounding him like silver confetti.

'You are an hourglass dolphin!' Jenny shouted at the sea creature which seemed to pirouette in mid-air, laughing as it splashed back into the ocean.

A few seconds later, she saw another. They were hard to tell apart, each one dark, with the white curved body colouring that gave the species its name. But Jenny soon decided there were four of them, keeping pace with the ship, darting in and out of the waves . . . and laughing with her.

Hourglass dolphins were among the rarest creatures in southern waters. Only a handful of scientists had ever seen one. And now there were four of them . . . playing with her ship. Playing with her.

'You are beautiful,' she called to the dolphins, laughing as they ducked and dived, full of the simple joy of being alive. The joy was contagious.

Jenny looked around her, but there were no other passengers on the sun deck. They were all inside, eating their sumptuous lunch. She should go and get them. Or at least tell the captain to make an announcement. That was what she was here for. And the other thing she should do was fetch her camera. So few photos of the hourglass dolphin had ever been taken. This was a career opportunity.

She hesitated, and looked down at the creatures taking a few more moments alone with them.

'Now, don't you lot go away!' she told them, and sprinted for the stairs.

★ ★ ★

The passenger from cabin 642 watched her go. He hadn't meant to spy on her, but the top deck where he had sought his own solitude overlooked the deck below. He'd seen her come out into the sunshine. Seen her leaning over the railing, and for one terrible moment, he'd thought she was going to jump. How well he knew that kind of despair. He'd opened his mouth to call to her ... to stop her, but then he'd heard her laugh. Her laugh had carried up to him on the sea air and curled its way into his very soul. The joy in that laughter was something he had not heard or felt for a very long time.

He held his breath as if to stop time.

When she turned for the stairs, he recognised her as the girl from the library.

'Jenny.' He remembered. At the time he'd thought her a pretty girl — but he had long since become immune to pretty girls.

He closed his eyes recalling the sound of her laugh and the way her dark hair had danced in the wind. He had almost felt her pleasure as the dolphins broke through the water. It was as if a promise of light had flared after far too long in the darkness.

He felt it then — the emotion . . . the urge he hadn't felt in such a long time. His fingers ached with it. He opened his eyes, looking out over the waves. The dolphins were gone. He had to go too. Now. Before he lost that feeling. He had to get below before she returned with people around her to break the spell. He turned and walked quickly away.

★   ★   ★

Jenny sprinted back up the stairs, her camera in her hand. Karl was a few steps behind her. If the dolphins were still there, he would make an announcement over the ship's intercom, calling the passengers to witness the rare sight. Jenny was bubbling over with excitement, but as she reached deck six, she glanced down the corridor, past the passenger cabins towards the rear of the ship. This passing glance had become a habit these past few days, and this time, she was rewarded. She missed her footing, and stumbled.

'Are you all right?' Karl reached out a steadying hand.

'Yes. Fine.' Jenny risked another quick glance down the corridor, but the figure she'd seen had vanished through the door into the owner's cabin. Damn! She didn't have time to give it any more thought, she darted up the rest of the stairs and out onto the sun deck. Pulling her camera from its case, she took up her previous position on the ship's rail, thinking as she did how much more exciting marine biology was in the field, rather than the university.

Maybe when she returned from this cruise, she should rethink her career choice.

'Where . . . ' Karl said beside her.

'Just here. Alongside the ship,' Jenny replied, her eyes searching the waves for the tell-tale curve of a fin or a sleek body.

They waited for two minutes. Three. After five minutes, Jenny let her camera fall in disappointment. 'They must have gone.'

'That's a shame.'

'They really were here, Karl,' Jenny said. 'Hourglass dolphins. Honestly!'

'Hey. I believe you,' Karl said. 'If we're lucky, they might come back. If nothing else, it's a good omen at the start of the trip.'

'I guess so.' Jenny felt her mood slipping.

'Cheer up,' Karl said as he walked away.

Jenny took one last glance out to sea, hoping against hope that her rare friends had returned. Nothing. Her only companions were the ever-present gulls, circling in the wake of the ship.

8

Lian clutched the side of the toilet bowl, feeling the sweat trickle slowly down her spine. So, this must be morning sickness. It had absolutely nothing to recommend it. Slowly she rose from her knees. She turned around and sat down on the toilet until her knees and her hands stopped shaking. Then she slowly got up and walked out of the cubicle. She turned on a tap, running cold water into the sink. She splashed the water over her face, washing away the sweat and the tears. Then she reached for paper towels.

What was she doing being ill in a public toilet on a ship in the middle of the ocean? She should be safe at home, in her bed. With her own bathroom. One that didn't move in such a disconcerting way. She hunched her shoulders as the feeling swept over her again, but this time she didn't need to dash back into the cubicle.

When Lian finally emerged from the bathroom, she decided there was no way she was taking part in any shore excursion today. Quite apart from the fact that she felt weak and shaky, there was also the rather disconcerting issue of riding a small boat from the ship to the shore. In her present condition, she didn't think that was such a good idea. Instead, she headed for the public lounge on deck five. She declined the steward's offer of coffee and muffins, asking instead for iced water, which was duly delivered. She settled herself into a comfortable chair. She needed to rest and relax, but instead found herself unusually restless. She fiddled with a pile of paper napkins, traced the water droplets as they dribbled down the outside of her frosty glass and listened for the sounds of other people moving around the ship, hoping the sound of other voices would stop her feeling so terribly alone.

As the island came into view through the big glass observation windows, Lian turned her attention to that bleak shore. The lecture yesterday had been far more interesting that she'd expected, with tales of shipwrecked sailors, whalers and seal hunters, feral cats and rats and scientific research. Jenny, the lecturer, had made it all sound fascinating. Not only that, Lian had sat with Vera for the talk, and the older woman's asides had kept Lian giggling into her hand. She had no idea why Vera had such an interest in bloodstains and shipwrecks.

As if called by Lian's thoughts, Vera suddenly appeared, clutching her ever-present purple bag.

'Hello Lian,' she said as she approached. 'Are you all right, dear? You look a little frail.'

'I'm feeling a bit ill,' Lian said. 'It must be seasickness,' she added quickly. Vera was a sweet thing, but Lian wasn't going to tell her about her condition. Colin was going to be the first person she told. That was the whole point of this journey.

'You are going ashore, aren't you?' Vera asked. 'It would be such a shame to miss out. It all sounded very interesting.'

'I don't know that I'm up to hiking across the hills,' Lian said. 'I wouldn't want to hold everyone up.'

'I'm not planning any hiking either,' Vera said. 'I thought I'd just stroll around and look at the old buildings. Maybe we'll see a bit of one of the old wrecked ships. Nothing too adventurous. Why don't you come with me? We can keep each other company while the rest go stomping off into the wilds.'

That seemed a very good idea. What seemed less of a good idea was that the inflatable boat that was going to take them ashore.

'It's perfectly safe,' they were assured by the seaman waiting on deck two to help them board the Zodiac through what appeared to be nothing more than a hole in the ship's hull. The little boat was bobbing up and down in the water beside the ship in a most disconcerting fashion.

'Let me help you,' said a voice at Lian's side.

Lian was pleased to see Jenny Payne. The presence of someone from the expedition staff would be very reassuring.

'Jenny, Lian's feeling a bit . . . seasick,' Vera offered helpfully. 'And she's not altogether sure about the boat.'

'Neither was I, the first time,' Jenny confided with a wink. 'But it's easy. Just follow me.'

Lian took a deep breath and did as she was told. She scrambled down into the boat, taking her seat along the side. Her fingers closed around the rope that was there for just that purpose. She was slightly ashamed to see Vera clamber aboard the boat with more ease than she had managed. She really was quite amazing for someone her age. Jenny joined them and they set off. The journey to the pebble beach must have lasted only a few minutes, but by the time they got ashore, Lian definitely wasn't feeling much like hiking. Some sort of park ranger was waiting for them. He looked young and fit and eager, and immediately started talking about heading off along the shoreline to visit a penguin colony. Lian wasn't that fond of penguins.

'I'll stay here, if that's all right,' she said.

Not only did Vera stay with her, but Jenny also. Apparently the rules required one of the ship's team to be with them at all times. The rest of the group set out down the shoreline, listening to the enthusiastic guide's descriptions of the mating habits of the 850,000 pairs of royal penguins. Lian, Vera and Jenny strolled slowly towards the cluster of tumbled down buildings.

'This island used to be a hunting ground for sealers,' Jenny said, 'and penguin hunters. They used to boil down the penguins for their oil in these things.'

As Jenny pointed out the rusty iron boilers, Lian felt her stomach heave again and sweat break out on her forehead.

'I don't think Lian is particularly keen on that topic of conversation right now,' Vera interrupted Jenny.

'I think I just need to sit down for a minute.' Lian dropped onto a nearby rock with relief. 'I guess I'm just having trouble getting my sea legs.'

'If you say so, dear.'

Vera was looking at her with such sympathy, that Lian suddenly burst into tears.

'There, there.' The older woman sat next to her and put an arm around her shoulders. 'It's all right.'

'I don't know why I'm crying,' Lian sobbed. 'I'm all right. Really.'

'Of course you are,' Vera said. 'It's only your hormones playing up. It happens a lot when you're pregnant.'

'You're pregnant?' Jenny sounded shaken. Not judgemental but as if somehow the news startled her.

Lian felt another surge of tears in her eyes. 'How . . . How did you know?' she asked Vera.

'My dear, I have four children and nine grandchildren,' Vera said quite matter-of-factly. 'I should know a pregnancy when I see one.'

Lian sniffled a couple of times. 'I wanted Colin to be the first person I told,' she said.

'And he will be,' Vera exclaimed. 'You didn't tell me anything. I just figured it out.'

Lian almost smiled.

'Colin — that's your husband?' Jenny asked.

'Fiancé,' Lian corrected, telling herself it wasn't a lie. He would be as soon as he knew. 'He's with a research station on Antarctica. He signed up to winter on the ice as electrician, plumber, lab tech and general maintenance man.'

'Winter on the ice?' Vera raised her eyebrows. 'Now that sounds interesting.'

'It meant a long time apart — but the money is good,' Lian said. 'Enough to set us up with our own place. So we can get married . . . It seemed a good idea at the time.' She felt the despair coming back.

'And it still is a good idea,' Vera said cheerfully. 'But he doesn't know about the baby.'

'No. That's why I had to come. If I didn't come now, I wouldn't see him until after the baby is born . . . and I want . . . I want . . . ' The words just didn't come.

'Of course you want to get married before the baby is born,' Vera finished for her. 'There's nothing wrong with that.'

Lian turned to look up at the other two. 'And we will get married. I just know he'll be thrilled about the baby. We talked about having a family . . . eventually.'

Jenny didn't say anything. She looked slightly discomforted by the whole conversation, but Lian didn't really have the energy to wonder why. 'The captain will marry us — won't he?' Lian asked.

Jenny shrugged. 'I honestly don't know. I don't even know if it's legal.'

'We can soon find out,' Vera assured her, squeezing her shoulders again. 'Don't you worry.'

Lian nodded and sniffled a bit, but she did feel a certain sense of relief. 'You know,' she said and smiling at Vera, 'it's nice to have someone to talk to about it. It's been pretty hard being all on my own.'

'You didn't tell your parents?' Jenny asked.

'God, no!' Lian exclaimed. 'They'd be horrified. They don't even know about Colin. They're a bit old fashioned. Well . . . he's not Chinese. They are going to be so angry when they find out.'

'No they won't,' Vera cut in. 'They'll be excited and happy with the thought of a grandchild. Just you wait. They will be there when you need them.'

'I'm not so sure . . . ' Lian said.

'I am. Nine grandchildren . . . remember?'

Vera certainly was a comfort, and it did feel good to have it out in the open. It was also probably a very good idea that someone on the ship knew. In case . . . well in case she had any problems on the journey.

The three sat in silence for a while, enjoying the sunshine.

*　*　*

Jenny kept her eyes out to sea, where the *Cape Adare* floated serenely at anchor. She felt less than serene. Why was she suddenly surrounded by pregnant women? Well, not surrounded by them, but coming across two in just a few days was more than she was used to. First there was the vice chancellor's daughter. It was much easier to think of her like that than as Ray's fiancée. And now Lian. Pushing all thoughts of the first quickly aside, Jenny glanced sideways at Lian. Although they were probably about the same age, Lian looked about seventeen. It was partly her gorgeous skin, now a little puffy with crying and partly because she was so tiny. She also had an air of vulnerability that made her seem very, very young. No wonder Vera had decided to take the girl under her wing. Still, that was probably a good thing. The more time she spent with Vera, the more she liked her. The older woman was really very kind. She had a wonderful sense of humour and a lightning fast mind. Jenny just wished she knew why Vera had such a passion for blood and gore, murder and mayhem. There was also that huge purple bag, and the notebook. What was that all about?

The sound of an engine cut through the otherwise quiet day. Another Zodiac was coming ashore with more of the passengers. Jenny watched the passengers wade through the gently lapping waves onto the beach. They milled around chatting to their guide before setting out in the direction of the penguin colony. She tried not to feel disappointed.

'I don't think he's coming,' Vera said. 'He doesn't seem to want much company.'

'Who?' Lian wanted to know.

'There's a very attractive gentleman just above me, in the big suite,' Vera answered. 'Jenny is rather taken with him.'

'I'm not . . . '

'And that's not surprising,' Vera continued before Jenny could finish her statement, 'I've met him and he is very handsome.'

'When did you meet him?' Jenny was shocked to discover she felt almost jealous.

'Well, perhaps met is the wrong word,' Vera confessed with an almost cheeky smile. 'Yesterday morning, before breakfast, I saw him coming out of the observation lounge. Very early.'

'How early?'

'The sun was just rising,' Vera said. 'Perhaps he'd spent all night in there? He left this behind.'

Jenny and Lian exchanged a puzzled glance as Vera dived into her bag. After a couple of minutes digging about, she retrieved a folded paper napkin. She spread it open in her lap. Jenny looked at the drawing.

'Wow. That's good,' she said. 'Do you think he did that?'

'I think so,' Vera said. 'I wonder if it's his hand.'

'Wait a second,' Lian said. 'I think . . .'

Now it was Vera's turn to look puzzled as Lian dug into the pockets of her coat. She laid a paper napkin in her own lap. 'Snap.'

There was no doubt they had both been drawn by the same artist. Where Vera's showed a hand and a skull ring, the drawing in Lian's lap was of part of a man's face, drawn almost in profile. It was an angular face, a little cruel perhaps, but still compelling. The eyes were just empty triangles, giving the impression that the man was wearing some kind of mask. Although both drawings had been made with an ordinary grey pencil, the texture of the paper, and the skill of the artist gave the impression of many shades of light and dark.

'Where did you find yours?' Vera asked.

'In the passenger lounge. It was on the floor. He must have dropped it.'

'Wow.' Jenny reached out as if to touch the drawings, but her hand stopped, hovering just a millimetre above the soft tissue. 'Why would he draw this?'

'It's obvious,' said Vera. 'He's a criminal. Look at the skull ring. The mask. Your gorgeous man is on the run from the law . . . that's why he's on the cruise. He's hiding.'

'No . . . ' Jenny exclaimed.

'Maybe he's a vampire,' Lian interjected.

'A vampire?' Jenny found that even sillier.

'Well, no one ever sees him,' argued Lian. 'He only comes out at dark. He's a vampire.' She held up the drawing of the haunted face. 'This is a *jiāngshī*. The dead who walk the earth sucking the life from mortals.'

'Oh, please!' Jenny said. 'He's not a vampire.'

'Have you ever seen him in daylight?' Lian queried her.

'Well, no. But . . . '

'And Vera saw him heading back to his cabin at dawn. That proves it.'

'That doesn't prove anything,' Jenny continued to defend the poor man's reputation. 'For all we know, he could be lying in the sun on his private balcony right now.'

All three of them glanced over to where the ship lay at anchor. The bow was facing away from them, and they could clearly see the balconies. The lower was the restaurant. Above that, deck five. Vera had one of those balconies. Above her, one large balcony across the back of the ship was the owner's private space.

'There is someone there,' Jenny said in a hushed tone, as if her voice might somehow carry over the water to alert him.

'You're right,' Lian said.

Over so great a distance, it was impossible to see any detail, but there was definitely movement on the balcony. And a dark shape.

'So maybe he's not *jiāngshī*. I wish the ship wasn't so far away. I'm the only one here who hasn't seen our mystery man.'

'Just a moment,' Vera once more opened her bag, 'I should have . . . ah ha!' She produced a black object and held it up triumphantly.

Jenny watched her open the small leather pouch and remove . . . 'Binoculars?'

'You just never know when you might need them,' Vera said, putting them to her eyes. 'Just give me a minute. Hmm — it's still a bit too far to see much.'

'Let me see.' Lian held out her hand.

'There's definitely someone on the balcony,' Vera explained to Jenny as Lian peered through the binoculars. 'You really can't see him very well in the shadows. I think he's just standing there, staring out to sea.'

'He's hiding from the daylight.' Lian fiddled with the focus. 'Waiting for the night to come so he can go in search of blood.'

'Stop that,' Jenny chided, trying not to laugh. 'And put those things away. It's not nice to pry like that.'

'But . . . '

'No. Lian,' Vera recovered her property. 'Jenny's right. It's a bit like being a stalker. And she is ship's crew — so we have to do what she says . . . unless . . . ' she turned to Jenny, the binoculars in her hand, 'unless you want a look, Jenny dear?'

Did she want to look? Of course she did. She hadn't been able to get him out of her mind. And now she was curious about just what was going on in the cabin. But . . .

'No!' she said firmly. 'Come on ladies, we'd better behave ourselves.' She ruefully watched Vera put the binoculars back into her bag.

9

The ocean was becoming very rough. Jenny clutched the hand rail tightly as she headed up the outside stairs towards the observation area on deck eight. She was supposed to remind anyone up there that there was a lecture in the lounge. Not that she expected to find anyone. With the stormy seas and falling temperatures, night time strolls on the open deck were not what they had once been. Karl's lecture on the early exploration of Antarctica inside the warm observation lounge, with bar service, was a much more inviting prospect. The lecture focused on the lives and gruesome deaths of the explorers, and Jenny expected Vera would be in the front row, pen in hand. There was something niggling the back of her mind about Vera, and she couldn't figure out just what it was. She liked the older woman a lot, but there was something . . .

The ship lurched again and Jenny's feet slipped from under her. She reached out a hand to grab the railing, but another sudden change in the ship's motion broke her grip. With a yell of pain as her wrist twisted, she fell down the last few stairs, crashing into the metal deck below.

Her bum hurt. One leg was twisted in a most uncomfortable fashion and her wrist hurt like crazy. Oh yes, the deck was wet with sea spray that was seeping slowly through her clothes.

Jenny didn't swear often. Only in moments of extreme stress. For the third time since she boarded the *Cape Adare* — she let out a loud exclamation.

'Shit!'

'Are you all right?'

The voice came from somewhere above the expensive looking hiking shoes that had suddenly appeared on the deck just a few inches in front of

163

her. She looked up.

'Oh.'

'Let me help you.'

A strong hand reached down to her. Nursing her injured wrist, Jenny placed her good hand in his, and allowed him to pull her to her feet.

'Are you hurt?'

'I don't think so.'

He was still holding her hand, his strong fingers clasped around hers to steady her. His touch wasn't having quite the effect he was probably hoping for. In fact, quite the opposite.

'I guess I still have to work on my sea legs,' Jenny said.

'I guess so.' The brow above those disconcertingly blue eyes creased in concern as he looked her up and down. 'Are you sure you're all right. That was a nasty fall.'

'I'm sure, thanks.' As she spoke, the ship lurched again. Jenny was thrown against the ship's railing. Instinctively she grabbed for it with both hands, then yelled as searing pain shot from her injured wrist all the way up her arm.

'It's all right, I've got you.'

He did. His arm was around her, steadying her as she cradled her injured arm against her stomach.

'I think I must have hurt my wrist in the fall.' Her voice sounded a bit like the whimper of an injured animal.

'You think? Come on, let's get you to the sick bay.'

'I can manage on my own . . . ' Jenny started to protest.

'You probably can, but why should you, when I'm here to help?'

Keeping one arm firmly around her, he pushed open the heavy door as if it weighed nothing, and led her inside. The lobby area outside the observation lounge wasn't really any more stable than the deck outside. The thick blue carpet just offered better grip. A few hardy souls were heading for the lounge and Karl's lecture. They stopped in surprise as Jenny was helped though the door.

'Can someone please find a crew member? Ask them to find the doctor. We'll meet him in the sick bay.'

He brushed aside the sudden wave of questions.

'It's nothing serious. Jenny's hurt her wrist. We just need the doctor to check it as a precaution.'

He remembered her name!

As if by magic, a few seconds later they were in the lift and descending slowly and silently towards deck two and the sick bay. The lift, like the rest of the ship, was rocking in a most disconcerting manner, but Jenny braced herself in the corner.

'I don't know your name,' she said.

Before he could answer, the lift stopped and the doors slid open. The ship's doctor was standing there, waiting for them.

'What happened?' he asked as between the two of them they guided Jenny from the lift into the nearby sick bay.

'She fell on the outer stairs.'

The sick bay was bright and roomy.

To Jenny's left as they entered, were two small alcoves which would serve as rooms for patients. They had curtains, rather than doors. The curtains were pulled back to reveal empty beds. To the right was another curtained alcove. This was the treatment room. As the door closed behind Jenny, a familiar figure emerged from the doctor's office.

'Jenny! Are you all right?' Vera's face was creased with concern.

'I'm fine. It's just my wrist.' Jenny allowed herself to be settled on to a bed. 'Honestly, it's no big deal.'

'You let William be the judge of that,' Vera said.

'William?'

'That's me.' The doctor gently took her wrist and turned it over to examine it. 'Can you move your fingers?'

She could but it hurt.

'Just a sprain,' the doctor pronounced. 'I'll strap it for you. And we probably should put something on that scratch.'

'Scratch?' Jenny had no idea what he

was talking about.

'Your cheek, dear,' Vera offered helpfully.

Now she thought about it, Jenny became aware that her cheek was smarting. She touched it gently and saw a small stain of blood on her fingers as she took them away. 'How did that happen?'

'I think you scraped your face against the edge of the steps,' her rescuer offered. His lips had curved into a slight smile that made his face even more handsome. The sight of her blood had not caused him to suddenly sprout fangs, which further disproved Lian's vampire theory.

Silence settled on the small group in the sick bay as the doctor tended to Jenny's cheek.

'Well, I think you're in safe hands now.' Her rescuer was leaving!

'Thank you for helping me ... ' Jenny paused, giving him a chance to tell her his name.

'You are very welcome,' he said as he vanished.

Jenny stared after him.

'Why won't you tell me your name?' she asked the closing door.

*   *   *

The owner's suite was by far the most luxurious place on board the *Cape Adare*, designed and outfitted for people with money, who appreciated the very best of everything.

It was U-shaped and spanned the full width of the ship, as did the balcony on the other side of the huge picture windows. The bathroom which sat in one arm of the U was small, but the towels were thick and soft. The bed was the largest on the ship, much bigger than even the captain's bunk, and it was liberally dotted with thick feather pillows. The carpet in the cabin was a similar blue to that in the public areas, but it was deeper and richer. There was a sofa, a comfortable arm chair and a dining table with four chairs. A closer look at the furniture would reveal the subtle but sturdy fixtures that held the pieces to the floor, to keep it stable in even the roughest seas.

As well as the standard tea and coffee making facilities, there was a bar fridge, well stocked, and some fine crystal glasses. Once again, all were suitably fixed in place with soft leather straps. Except for one fine crystal glass, which was in the hand of the man who stood on the balcony.

He hadn't really noticed the quality of the crystal. Such things meant little to him. He had, however, noticed the quality of the dark amber liquid inside the glass, and he sipped it slowly, savouring the taste. The movement of the ship caused the dark amber liquid inside the glass to slosh about, but not a drop was spilled. The passenger had good balance — but he also had one hand on the railing that lined not only this balcony, but every part of the ship. One hand for you, one hand for the ship. It was a seafaring maxim, and this passenger had taken good note of it. He wasn't about to fall down any stairs.

'Why didn't I tell her my name?' he asked the empty night.

The answer was simple — habit. The desire to preserve his privacy had become a need for anonymity so strong that giving out his name was almost like breaking a sacred taboo.

He could simply have told her his name was Christopher, which it was. He might even have said Christopher Walker. She would never have recognised it. But no one called him Christopher. He had been Kit since he was a boy. Would she know who Kit Walker was? Possibly. It was better that he kept his secret.

He took another sip of scotch, feeling the spirit gently warm his throat. They were a long way south now, it was getting colder. The wind on his face was so cold it was almost painful. He welcomed it, just as he welcomed the images flashing inside his head and the desire that was making his fingers twitch.

He turned back inside the cabin. Closing out the cold and the wind and the night. On the starboard side of his cabin, a selection of boxes and packages had been stowed, securely fixed against the sort of weather they were now beginning to encounter. Only one of those packages had been opened. He'd done that during the quiet hours at the island. He'd run his hands over the dark polished wood that was so familiar to him it was like a part of his body — but had of late been a stranger. He'd even gone so far as to take it onto the balcony, ready for him. But when they'd departed the island, he'd packed it away safely again. He still couldn't take that step.

In another couple of days, after they had crossed the wild southern ocean, the seas would become almost glassy. At that point, should he wish, he could open all those boxes. Although he'd gone to great pains to bring everything he might need, he hadn't really thought he would unwrap those packages. It had been two years since . . .

He swallowed the last of the scotch. Two years was a long time. He put the glass down and stared at his hands, turning them slowly over to study the lines on his palms. They were such ordinary hands. What if he couldn't do it anymore? What if his hands had lost their magic when his heart broke?

No. He wouldn't believe that. He couldn't believe that. This trip was supposed to free him from that terrible prison of his own making. He closed his eyes dreading the darkness that had haunted him for so long. But this time, the darkness didn't come. For the first time in so many agonising months, there was light waiting for him. A soft golden light. Warm and welcoming. And in the light, he saw a girl who talked to dolphins. His fingers began to tingle. Without pausing to ask why or how . . . he welcomed the gift and ripped open one of the packages.

★　★　★

'He's right above us, you know,' Vera said in a conspiratorial tone.

'Who is?' Jenny asked, although she knew very well who Vera was talking about. He was on her mind too.

'Your mysterious friend and rescuer,' Vera said. 'Now, how do you have your tea?'

Jenny sank back into the sofa with a sigh. Her wrist was firmly strapped, and the scratch on her face had been bathed and pronounced not life-threatening. Vera had insisted that Jenny accompany her to her suite, for a restorative cup of tea. On the way, they had bumped into Lian, sitting quietly in a corner and looking a little sad. Vera had gathered the girl up as they passed, declaring that the three of them would all enjoy a nice girlie chat and a good cup of tea. There had also been mention of biscuits.

'How nice, to be rescued like that,' Lian sighed. 'Although it is a shame he's not a vampire.'

'Never mind,' Jenny said, grinning.

'Maybe next time.'

'You know, he still could be a criminal,' Vera said, clattering mugs around as she made their drinks. 'Otherwise, why didn't he tell you his name?'

'There could be a perfectly good reason,' Jenny leaped to his defence.

'Such as?' Lian challenged.

'Maybe . . . ' Jenny mentally groped for an answer. 'Maybe he's famous. A famous actor . . . '

'But we'd recognise him!' Lian protested.

'An author then. Someone we might have heard of, but wouldn't recognise.'

Behind Jenny, Vera suddenly dropped a cup.

'Let me help you.' Lian got to her feet, staggering just a little with the movement of the ship as she went to help.

Vera's suite was about three times the size of the tiny crew cabins, and far more luxurious. Jenny sank back into the seat, enjoying the chance to just relax, and let someone else do the organising.

'By the way,' she said. 'Why were you down with the doctor when I arrived, Vera? You weren't feeling seasick were you?'

'Good heavens, Jenny. Do I look like the sort who gets seasick?'

Jenny had to admit she didn't.

'I was having a lovely chat to him about the effect of extreme cold on the libido.'

Jenny raised an eyebrow as Lian stifled a giggle. Was Vera worried that the cold was going to turn the men on board into sex-crazed monsters . . . or maybe it was herself she was worried about.

'And what did he say?' Jenny had to ask as she accepted a steaming cup from Lian.

'He didn't seem to have much information.' Vera shook her head in puzzlement. 'I shall have to google it.'

'Well, hopefully, it won't deter Jenny's rescuer,' Lian said, grinning.

'Stop it!' Jenny protested, but she couldn't stop her eyes from glancing upward towards the deck above and the owner's cabin, where right now, the mysterious passenger might be . . .

It was a good thing her thoughts were interrupted by a knock on the door. She didn't altogether like where the conversation was going.

Vera opened the door.

'Come in, Anna.' She stepped aside to let the expedition leader's wife enter the room.

'Hi, Jenny,' Anna said. 'How are you? The doctor said I'd find you here. I'm sorry I wasn't there to help earlier. I was off nursing some of the seasick passengers.'

'Don't worry about it,' Jenny said. 'I imagine you and the doctor have got more than enough on your plate, without worrying about me.'

'We soon will, I think,' Anna said.

'What do you mean?' Vera asked.

'Well, I guess it's all right to tell you,' Anna said. 'It will be all over the ship soon.'

'What will?'

177

'We're changing our heading,' Anna said. 'Because of the storm.'

Jenny nodded; there had been a lot of discussion earlier that day about a huge storm tearing through the ocean south east of their position.

'We're going around it?' It seemed the sensible thing to do.

'Not exactly,' Anna hesitated, then shrugged. 'You may as well know now . . . we're heading into it.'

'What!' Vera and Lian asked in unison.

'Why?' Jenny added.

'There's a yacht. A lone sailor on some round the world quest. He's in trouble. The yacht is sinking and we're the only ship close enough to attempt a rescue.'

'Isn't that dangerous?' Lian asked in a shaky voice. 'Surely the captain wouldn't risk this ship and everyone on board for just one man?'

'The *Cape Adare* is big enough to handle the storm,' Anna assured her. 'There's no real risk. There's also no real choice. The International Law of the Sea requires us to go to his rescue.'

'And it's the right thing to do,' Vera said.

'Yes. It is,' Anna agreed. 'We have to at least try to reach him.'

'And he's . . . ' Jenny had a feeling she already knew the answer.

'Right in the heart of the storm.'

10

The waves were truly terrifying.

In the observation lounge, Lian gripped the sides of her chair, while the *Cape Adare* fought her way into the storm. The foaming water crashed over the bow of the ship as she plunged into another giant wave. Lian closed her eyes as the ship rolled from side to side. If it was like this for a big ship like the *Cape Adare*, how must it be for a small yacht . . . and a man alone on that yacht?

'Cor! Imagine being out there in that.'

Lian glanced up. Several of the English lads had wandered into the lounge. Well, staggered would be a better word as they lurched with the rolling of the ship, grabbing on to whatever looked solid enough to stabilise them. A couple of them looked a little green around the gills. Lian wondered if they knew that the ship's doctor was handing out seasickness pills as if they were sweeties. Strangely enough, with the onset of the storm, her own stomach had settled — it was as if the morning sickness had retreated in the face of far bigger concerns.

She rested her hand on her stomach and thought about the new life starting there. The new life that she was supposed to protect and nurture. Yet here she was on a ship that was driving headfirst into a terrifying storm. She wasn't afraid that the ship would sink. If there was any danger of that, the captain would turn the ship around. Wouldn't he? She was more afraid of what might happen if she lost her balance on the heaving deck. Would a fall harm her? Harm her baby? She had no idea. What was she doing? She needed help. She couldn't face this alone.

'I bet we don't find him . . . ' The speaker's voice trailed off as the deck heaved, sending him running across the lounge to end up gripping a rail. His friends laughed, while maintaining a firm grip on anything nearby that was stable.

'He's probably already gone under.'

Lian wasn't trying to eavesdrop. They were just talking very loudly.

'I heard someone say the bridge had been talking to him on the radio.'

That wasn't quite right. Jenny had told her they were tracking a radio distress beacon that must be on board the stricken yacht. Lian tried to imagine how the yachtsman must feel. Alone in those mountainous seas. How frightened he must be. Was he making his peace with whatever God he believed in? Was he still fighting for survival, or had he given up and resigned himself to joining Davy Jones down below?

'Hello.' A young male voice spoke close to her side. 'Remember me?'

'Us, you imbecile. She should remember us.'

'Well, some of us, anyway.'

Lian was once again surrounded by eager young faces and English accents.

'Hi guys,' she said. She didn't want to be rude, but she wasn't really in the mood for them.

The ship rolled again, and the lads caught hold of each other, and her chair, to stop themselves being thrown across the room.

'Isn't this exciting,' the tall one said happily. 'Just think. We're going to be heroes.'

'Not you mate,' one of his companions gave him a not-so-gentle punch in the shoulder. 'You're just a witness.'

'Hey, maybe we can get interviewed by the BBC,' the first youth offered. 'Mr Barstow, can you tell us exactly what happened?' he intoned in a deep voice.

'Why would anyone want to talk to you,' his shorter friend said, 'when they have a chance to talk to someone much nicer and far better looking?' He focused his attention back on Lian

Lian smiled. She couldn't help

herself. She was only a couple of years older than these boys, but she felt almost motherly towards them. Must be more hormones, she guessed.

'Hello boys, isn't this exciting!' Vera's arrival effectively released Lian from the obligation to respond. She dropped into a vacant chair and placed her handbag securely in her lap. She seemed remarkably unruffled by the wild seas and the ship's movement. 'Hopefully we'll get a good view of the rescue from here.'

'That would be cool!'

Vera leaned over towards Lian, and patted her hand gently. 'You know boys,' she said in a sweet voice, 'a lot of people are having trouble with the weather. Seasick you know. It's all the heaving and tossing of the ship.'

Lian saw one boy's face turn a slightly more obvious shade of green.

'Of course, I imagine it will take more than a few waves to have you strong young things with your heads down the toilet bowl,' Vera continued innocently. 'It's a good thing the doctor has seasickness pills for those who need them.'

'He has?' The young male voice was decidedly shaky.

'He certainly does. He's handing them out to everyone. But of course you don't need them, do you?'

Lian chuckled quietly as the boys exchanged glances.

'Well,' the one called Barstow said. 'I guess it wouldn't hurt to have some, just in case one of the other lads felt poorly.'

'Yes. That's a good idea,' agreed his green-tinged companion. 'After all, we wouldn't want them to miss the rescue . . . because they are . . . ' He broke off in mid-sentence and darted away. His friends followed, breaking into a semi-run as the ship rolled again.

'Oh dear,' said Vera. 'Not very strong of stomach are they?'

Lian grinned. 'I guess not.'

'What about you my dear, how are you coping with the weather?'

'The weather is fine really,' Lian said. 'But . . . '

Lian looked at Vera's kind face, and felt that she just wanted to burst into tears. She gulped the feeling down. 'It's a little bit scary though,' she said.

'Don't you worry,' Vera said, her voice brimming with confidence. 'William — that's the doctor — tells me the ship has been through far worse than this. And the captain is very experienced. He hasn't lost a ship yet!'

Instead of giggling as Vera had no doubt intended, Lian suddenly felt tears running down her face. 'Oh Vera, what on earth am I doing here? I'm frightened. Really frightened. Not for me. For my baby. What on earth possessed me to do this?'

'You are taking your baby to meet his — or her — father. You're going to give your young man the very best news in the world. You are doing the right thing.'

'But it's not supposed to be like this.' Lian waved her arms to take in the room, and the groups of passengers who were clinging tight to every stable surface while watching the huge seas. 'I always used to imagine what it would be like. Having a baby. Telling my husband. My parents. I used to dream about the things we would do to welcome a new member of the family. But . . . it's . . . ' Her voice trailed off.

'It's not like you imagined? Goodness, dear. Having a baby never is. It's the most unpredictable thing on the planet. Why, I realised I was pregnant with my first when I fainted in a graveyard.'

'A graveyard?'

'Yes. I keeled over right next to a grand marble mausoleum. My poor husband thought I'd died. It was so unlike me to faint in such a fascinating place.'

'You husband is . . . ' Lian wasn't quite sure how to frame the question.

'Gone? Sadly, yes.' Vera anticipated her. 'Five years ago now. Heart attack.'

'Oh, I'm sorry.'

For a few seconds Vera's eyes clouded over and the ever-present smile dimmed just a fraction. Then she took a deep breath. 'I do still miss him you know. We were married for more than forty years.'

'Wow.' Lian was impressed. 'That's wonderful.'

'Yes. Yes, it was,' Vera said. 'And it will be for you too, my dear. Don't you worry.'

Lian nodded, surprised to find her fear had faded. They sat in silence for a few minutes as the boat continued its brave struggle into the storm. Every few seconds, the deck heaved and tossed beneath their chairs, which were securely bolted to the floor.

'I am beginning to understand the way they've decorated this place,' Vera finally said.

'What do you mean?'

'Well, these chairs, with the high sides. Without them, we'd be tossed on the floor every few seconds.'

At that moment, a sudden burst of brilliant white light exploded in the sky directly in front of the ship.

'What was that?' Lian asked, blinking.

'A flare,' a voice said as Jenny staggered up and sat down next to them. 'One of ours.'

'Have they spotted him?' Vera asked.

'Not yet. But we're close to where he should be. That's why they're sending up flares. Hopefully he'll respond.'

'What happens then?' Vera asked.

'I'm not entirely sure.' Jenny stood up. Her injured wrist was still strapped, but with the other she took a firm hold on the back of her seat for balance and raised her voice to address all the assembled passengers.

'As you have probably worked out, we're getting close to the yacht's expected location,' she told the silent room. 'Can I ask you all please to stay here in the observation lounge. Don't go out on deck. Apart from the fact that it's dangerous out there in these heavy seas, our crew need to focus all their efforts on that yacht. We don't want to have to go fishing for passengers as well.'

The last line brought a small laugh.

'How are they going to save him?' someone asked.

'They're experienced seamen,' Jenny said. 'They'll know what to do.' She dropped back into her chair.

'I hope so,' Lian said softly as she stared out through the glass at the angry ocean.

11

Was death out there — among the waves?

Kit gripped the railing with both hands, struggling to remain upright as the ship heaved beneath him like some dying leviathan. Freezing windswept water stung his face, but it was impossible to know if it was the driving rain or the spray from the waves that crashed across the bow of the ship every few seconds. He shouldn't be out in the open. Even in this most sheltered spot on the top deck, surrounded on three sides by a high glass wall, he wasn't safe. One freak wave; one unexpected movement of the deck and he could be lost — as lost as the tiny yacht that was out there somewhere in the raging ocean. Only a fool would stand here. A fool or a man with nothing left to lose.

He should join the other passengers in the warm safety of the viewing lounge. They were so caught up in the drama of the rescue attempt, they wouldn't recognise him. They probably wouldn't even notice him. But he just couldn't do it.

Had it come to this? That he would rather stand alone, freezing and in danger than face other people. If so, he was already lost.

The *Cape Adare* was struggling in the mountainous seas. It was early afternoon, but the threatening dark clouds were so thick and low, they obscured the sun, leaving the ship in grey twilight. An hour ago, in one of his regular updates, the captain had informed his passengers that the storm was abating. If that was true, it was doing it very slowly. The captain had also said they were still receiving the distress signal from the yacht. That meant it was still afloat. Was the crew still alive?

At that moment, the sky above the

ship exploded with a white light so bright, it almost hurt to look at it. The *Cape Adare* had sent up a flare. If there was anyone alive out there in that cruel ocean, they would see it. Kit held his breath.

The ship lurched suddenly, and Kit slipped on the wet deck. Only his knuckle-white grip on the railing kept him from sliding towards the edge of the deck, and the turbulent ocean beyond. He hauled himself back to his feet, and as he did, the sky burst into light again. But this time, the light was red — and distant.

Someone on the crippled yacht had set off a distress flare.

The *Cape Adare* was heaving so greatly in the sea, it was impossible to see if there was anything out there as the flare slowly fell back towards the hungry waves. It vanished, and Kit wondered if the chance of a rescue had vanished with it. He stared out into the raging water.

There was something out there!

Wiping water from his eyes, Kit looked again. It was gone . . . no. A rising wave lifted the *Adare* and not too far away, Kit saw a pale shape slide down the face of the next wave. It was the yacht — but barely recognizable. The mast was gone. A shattered timber stump was all that remained. The deck of the little sailing boat was littered with the remains of the rigging and railings, torn and twisted by the sea. But, clinging desperately to the shattered remains and totally at the mercy of the wild water, was a man. He was dressed in a bright orange survival suit, his safety harness the only thing stopping the waves from claiming him. But that safety line posed a danger too. If the boat sank, the man would be dragged down with it.

A huge wave crashed over the yacht and it vanished. Kit gave an involuntary yell as the man was swallowed by the dark grey water. He strained forward then saw the little yacht bravely claw its way out of the wave, the man still clinging to the remains of the mast. The boat was very low in the water. It didn't have much time left.

Something moved on the deck of the *Adare*. Kit glanced down. Four seamen were on deck, struggling towards the bow of the ship, their lifelines trailing behind them. They gathered around what looked like some sort of harpoon.

There was no sound — but Kit saw the rope snake out towards the crippled yacht. Kit strained to see where it fell. The man on the yacht held up one arm . . . signalling failure. The seamen on the *Adare* swung into action, preparing a second line.

Such a struggle for survival. Such determination.

Kit's throat caught. Had Dana struggled to survive? Or had she welcomed the darkness as an end to her pain? Could he have saved her if only he'd found her in time? He would never know . . .

The second lifeline shot towards the

crippled yacht, and Kit saw the man in the survival suit lunge for it. As he did, the little yacht ceased its slow climb up the rising wave. It shuddered and began to slip backwards. The battle was over. The time left to the man on the yacht could be measured in seconds. He fumbled with the rope.

Kit held his breath, willing the man to keep fighting. Don't give in, he wanted to shout. Don't let the darkness take you. Keep fighting.

As the little yacht began to slip stern first towards the ocean floor, her captain flung himself into the wild water.

*   *   *

An audible gasp filed the observation lounge.

'He's gone overboard!' someone said in a voice that quivered with something approaching panic.

'Did he get the lifeline?' someone else asked.

Jenny didn't know the answer. Like the passengers, she was glued to the life and death struggle that was all too clearly visible from the observation lounge. Most of the passengers had been grumbling about the storm, and complaining about their own discomfort — until they had caught that first glimpse of the tiny yacht. In silence they had watched it battle for life. When the figure in the bright orange safety suit had staggered on deck — it suddenly became all too real. A man was dying out there. They were his only hope.

On the deck below, Jenny could see the crewmen, themselves wearing safety lines, hauling on the lifeline that vanished over the side of the ship into the heaving water. She looked out at the raging sea. How could anyone survive in that?

'Is that him?' someone cried, pointing out into the water. 'I saw something orange. It must be him.'

If it seemed like an eternity to those

watching, how must it feel to the man in the water? Jenny felt a hand grip hers. Safe in the high-sided seat beside her, Lian was trembling with anxiety. Vera was beside her, staring out into the ocean. For once, her pen and notebook were nowhere in evidence. A tense silence settled in the room, as everyone held their breath . . .

'Look!'

On the deck, the seamen were hauling an orange clad figure through a gap in the railing. A couple of people started to cheer, but fell immediately silent as the seamen lowered the motionless figure to the deck. The seamen stepped back.

'William,' Vera said quietly as the doctor bent over the stricken man. For a few seconds nothing happened and a terrible dread settled on Jenny. They had come too late.

Then there was a flurry of movement on the deck.

'He's alive. I saw him move!'

This time the cheer was deafening.

Two of the seamen below lifted the man from the deck. The small group vanished from sight into the ship.

12

The mood in the lounge was exuberant. The *Cape Adare* was rapidly drawing away from the storm. The ocean outside was far from smooth, but compared to the previous twenty-four hours, it was a millpond. No one had fallen over or dropped a glass for at least half an hour. But better than all that was the news that the rescued sailor was doing well. A short time ago, the captain had announced that their new guest was recovering from his ordeal. He'd be in the sick bay for a day or two under the doctor's care, but would soon be up and about. The captain had thanked everyone for their understanding and patience.

Jenny glanced around the room, noting the animated faces and lively conversation. It wasn't just that the pre-dinner cocktails were flowing. It was as if everyone felt a little pride at what their ship had done. As if they had played some small part in the rescue. And why not, she thought. That was a totally understandable and human reaction. There was, of course, one person who wasn't joining in. The mysterious passenger from cabin 642 was nowhere to be seen, as usual. Jenny wondered if he even knew about the rescue. He must. The whole ship knew. Not even someone who sought solitude could have ignored the event.

Perhaps tonight, now that the seas had dropped, she would go to the upper deck. While most of the passengers were celebrating after dinner, he might just . . .

'Hello, dear,' Vera's voice interrupted her thoughts. 'It's good news about that poor man.'

'It certainly is Vera,' Jenny replied.

'I wonder when he'd feel up to talking to me,' Vera said thoughtfully. 'There are so many questions I want to ask him. About what happened. What it was like out there.'

Jenny felt a flash of something approaching annoyance. While she found Vera refreshingly quirky, she doubted the rescued yachtsman would feel the same. 'I imagine he probably doesn't want to talk about it . . . ' she started to say.

'Nonsense,' Vera said firmly. 'People who set out on adventures like that always want to talk about it.'

Jenny wasn't so sure, but she was prevented from commenting by the dinner bell.

'Are you coming to dinner?' Vera asked.

'Soon.' Jenny said.

'If William is there, he may have some news about that poor man's condition,' Vera remarked as she set off in the direction of the restaurant.

Jenny watched her go, shaking her head. She wished she could remember what it was that made Vera seem somehow familiar. Whatever it was, thinking about it wasn't going to bring it back. Nodding hello to a few other passengers who were also heading towards the restaurant, Jenny made her way to the internet café. Now would be a good time to send that e-mail to her family. To admit she wasn't coming to Christmas dinner. She also had to confess about her job. But she'd do that in person when she got back.

She took a seat and logged in. She opened a new e-mail and stared at it for a few seconds before putting her fingers on the keyboard to begin typing.

It took her several attempts, but at last she hit the send key. That done, she decided she needed a bit of fresh air and headed upstairs to the open deck.

As she stepped through the door, the chilly wind grabbed her jacket and tore at it, threatening to pull it from her body. It was cold, and the storm wasn't giving up easily. Jenny considered going back to her cabin for some warmer clothing, then decided against it. After what that poor sailor had been through, the least she could do was handle a bit of a cold wind. A freezing wind, she corrected herself a few seconds later as she pulled her light jacket closer around her. She looked towards the stern. There should be some shelter behind the ship's funnel.

There was, and Jenny found herself enjoying both the solitude and the fresh air. The white tipped waves swirled in the ship's wake. Above her, the storm clouds were beginning to scatter, creating a kaleidoscope of black and blue and violet and green as they raced before the wind. Every few seconds, a shaft of sunlight would break through, only to be swallowed up again as the clouds swept on. Jenny took several deep breaths of air, colder and cleaner than any she had ever tasted before. Perhaps the spectre of death that had hovered so close just a short time ago had heightened her perceptions — but she could feel and taste and touch the beauty all around her.

The clouds directly above her suddenly parted, allowing a broad band of golden light to stream in from the sun above. In the midst of that beam of light, two shining silver shapes soared above the restless surface of the water.

'Wandering albatross,' Jenny whispered.

The birds rode the wind with ease and grace, their great wings stretched wide to guide their flight. Jenny held her breath, waiting, but the albatross had no need to flap their wings as lesser birds do. In perfect synchronisation, they rose and fell with the wind, perfectly at home riding the invisible waves of air.

Jenny felt tears prick her eyes as she watched them.

'At length did cross an Albatross, through the fog it came; as if it had been a Christian soul, we hailed it in God's name,' the deep voice quoted Coleridge softly beside her.

Jenny didn't need to turn around to see who it was. She was as aware of his presence as the birds soaring above her were aware of each other. She didn't speak, nor did her companion.

The birds drew closer to the ship. Jenny could almost imagine her own reflection in the dark soft circles of their eyes. And behind her, another shape. A tall dark figure complementing her, as the two great birds did each other. Wingtips almost touching, hearts beating together, the two albatross lifted effortlessly back into the sky.

'The wandering albatross can fly for years without returning to land,' Jenny said. 'They mate for life. Imagine that, just the two of them, alone on the ocean. Needing and wanting nothing else.'

'How lonely it must be when one is left behind.'

He spoke so softly that she barely heard the words, but the pain, the immense sadness and loss in the sound of his voice made her breath catch in her throat. Jenny dragged her eyes away from the birds to look at him. He was staring out over the ocean, his face a mask of pain. She wanted to reach out and touch him. Her hand had barely begun to move, when he spoke again.

'I wonder if any of them ever get a second chance.'

'I'm sure they do,' Jenny replied softly.

'It would seem to be a betrayal of the first . . . ' She knew he wasn't talking about the birds any more.

'No one who truly loved would want to see their loved one alone.'

The passenger from cabin 642 turned away from the birds, his eyes shining with unshed tears as he looked down at Jenny. She felt his grief wash over her. She took his unresisting hand in hers.

He started at her touch. Jenny didn't let go. She held his hand until he nodded slowly. In the sky above them, the two albatross wheeled and turned away from the ship and the two people holding hands as they watched them go.

The clouds closed out the shaft of sunlight, and Jenny shivered.

'You should go back inside,' she was

told. 'You're not dressed for this.'

'Are you coming?'

'No. I'll stay a few more minutes.' He was better protected against the cold in a heavy woollen jumper.

Jenny nodded and reluctantly turned away. She had taken only a single step, when a voice halted her.

'By the way, my name is Christopher Walker. People call me Kit.'

Jenny glanced back. He was smiling, but it was the saddest smile she had ever seen.

'It's nice to meet you, Kit.' She turned away and left him standing in the shelter of the tall grey funnel.

* * *

Kit felt the silence and solitude close in around him once again. Was she right? Could there be a second chance for him? And if so . . .

He allowed himself to feel a small flare of hope. Soon they'd be through the worst of the weather. As they approached the great southern continent, the sea would turn glassy, and he'd be able to unpack the rest of the boxes in his cabin. For the first time, he felt a twinge of impatience. His fingers itched to feel the smooth wood again. Each time he closed his eyes, colours and shapes swirled in the darkness.

It was time. He could feel that it was time. The sea was still too rough for him to work properly. But that didn't mean he couldn't make a start. He turned away from the ocean and began to almost run across the deck towards the stairs that led to his cabin, and those packages that held the best of him.

13

He wouldn't mind, Vera thought as she rode the lift down to deck two. She was sure he wouldn't mind. Especially now that he'd had a good night's rest. A quick chat was all she wanted. A few notes, while the memory was fresh in his mind and he could tell her what had happened out there. Describe his battle for survival. She also wanted to look in his face and try to understand his feelings. The man had almost died. And in such a way! No one would be left untouched by that. She didn't want to upset him, but his story was remarkable. This was a rare and precious opportunity that she did not want to waste.

As the lift settled onto the deck, Vera found herself hoping that William was on duty this morning. That nurse — Anna — had answered when she'd knocked on the door last night. A bit of a bossy one, that one. She had been perfectly polite, but she wasn't letting anyone through the door unless they had good reason. Perhaps if Vera had been bleeding from a gaping wound she might have made it past the she-wolf on guard and into the sick bay, but she wasn't even one hundred per cent sure about that.

If she was going to be totally fair, Vera could admit the woman was only doing her job. Protecting her patient. But surely no one needed protection from a grey-haired little old lady like her. She was totally harmless.

Vera heard the noise as she stepped from the lift. It sounded like someone sobbing. She looked around but the deck was empty. There were no passenger cabins here. Behind the lifts, secured doors led forward to the staff quarters. To her left was the tender lobby, and the gangway they had used to enter the Zodiac boat for their island excursion. It was tightly closed now, protection against the storm. In front of her was the door to the sick bay, and the stairs leading up to deck three — and the cheapest of the passenger cabins.

On the stairs . . .

'Lian! What's the matter, dear? Are you all right?'

The girl was seated at the bend in the stairs. Half way between two floors. Her head was buried in her hands, and she was sobbing. Vera reached her in just a few seconds, and placed her hand gently on the girl's sleek dark head.

'Lian?'

'I'm scared,' the girl's voice was muffled. 'I woke up this morning . . . and . . . on the sheets. And I'm having cramps. I'm scared for my baby.'

'You need to get to the doctor.'

'I know. I was . . . but . . . ' Lian raised her head and looked up, tears falling unchecked down her cheeks. 'I almost slipped on the stairs.'

Vera's heart went out to the terrified

girl. 'All right. Well I'm here now. I won't let anything happen to you. The sea is really smooth this morning. Look — the deck isn't moving at all. If you hang on to the rail, and hold my hand, you'll be just fine.'

'But . . . '

'No buts,' Vera insisted. 'Don't let this grey hair fool you. I'm a pretty tough old bird. Come on now, we can go as slowly as you like.'

Lian wiped a hand across her face and got to her feet. With one hand she clutched the stair rail and the other gripped Vera's hand so tightly, that the older woman wondered for a moment if her frail bones might break.

'There you go. Easy. Now just one step at a time.' Vera was certain Lian would be fine. Her problem wasn't physical weakness. The poor girl was just terrified. Vera mentally shook her head in wonder. What sort of parents must she have — if she was willing to face this journey alone, rather than tell them about her baby?

They reached the bottom of the stairs.

'Good girl. I knew you'd be fine,' Vera said cheerfully.

Lian nodded. Her sobs had subsided and she was already looking better.

'Thank you,' she said.

Vera kept hold of the girl's hand as they walked the few steps to the sick bay door. Vera knocked briskly. She was very pleased to see William's handsome face as the door opened.

'Hello Vera,' he said. 'I had a feeling you might drop by this morning.' His smile faltered when he looked at Lian's tear stained face. 'I think you'd better come in.'

As they entered the sick bay, Vera glanced quickly towards the patient 'rooms' on her right. Sure enough, one of the curtains was pulled half way across the alcove, shielding the person who lay in the bed. She caught some movement out of the corner of her eye as she helped Lian towards the treatment area at the other end of the sick bay.

'Don't go,' Lian said tremulously as Vera went to step aside.

'I won't be far,' she said. 'I'll just wait outside.'

She looked at William, but her friend had dropped into his professional mode and with a brief nod, he indicated she should give him and his patient some privacy. Vera obliged, and the curtain slid closed behind her.

Vera moved away from the curtain to give Lian the privacy she needed. And if that brought her a little closer to the bed where the rescued sailor lay . . .

'Hello.'

Vera turned towards the voice, which had the rasping timbre of Bob Dylan at his best.

'Hello,' she replied. 'Are you all right? Do you need anything?'

'No. I just heard you come in.'

It was natural for her to move to the centre of the room, from where she could see the man in the small alcove. He was sitting up in bed, and with a gesture, signalled her over.

'I don't mean to disturb you,' Vera said, meaning it.

'You're not. In fact, right now, I could use some company.'

Vera let the last of her guilt drop away.

'I'm Vera Horsley,' she said as she approached the bed. 'How are you doing?'

'I'm getting there.' The man in the bed pulled himself upright and sat back against the pillow. 'I'm Glen Stewart.'

In her youth, Vera had nursed a secret passion for Robert Redford, with his shock of sandy blond hair and cheeky grin. She loved his strong jaw, and the way his face creased when he smiled. Glen Stewart's face was burnt by the sun and wind. In places, the skin was peeling, but he had much the same look. He hadn't shaved for many days, and there were dark circles of exhaustion under his eyes. But those eyes were a brilliant blue, and despite the tiredness she could see in them, they still smiled at her. In her mental list of heroes, Robert Redford moved down a notch to make way for his lookalike.

Vera held out her hand, then stopped as she looked at Glen's hands. They were strong hands, weathered by sun and sea. They were also hands that had fought to live. One was bandaged, with slight stains where something, blood probably, had soaked into the dressing. The skin on his bare arms was burned by the sun and marred by dark bruises and dozens of small cuts and scrapes. Vera began to realise the magnitude of the ordeal he had faced.

'It's nice to meet you,' Vera said. 'Are you sure I can't get you anything?'

'No. But if you have a moment, I'd like some company.'

'Of course.' Vera pulled a chair to the side of the bed and sat down, but she found she could think of nothing to say. She, who had set out this morning determined to talk to this very man, was lost for words. It was something that had happened only rarely in her life.

'So — the doctor tells me you were heading for Antarctica,' Glen said at last.

'Yes. We detoured when we picked up your distress signal.'

'I'm very glad you did.' A dark shadow seemed to cloud Glen's eyes. 'If you hadn't . . .'

'You don't have to talk about it, you know,' Vera said hastily, despite the fact that she really wanted to know everything.

'It's all right. I imagine at some point someone will tell me it is a good thing to talk about it. And I guess they'll be right.'

'Were you in a race or something?' Vera asked.

'No. I set out from Perth to sail the Southern Ocean. I just wanted to see it. It was a challenge you see. Me and Peregrine . . . that was my yacht . . . against everything the Southern Ocean could throw at us. I guess I lost.' Glen's mouth twisted in a wry half-smile.

'I don't know about that,' Vera said. 'You're still alive. That has to count for something.'

When he didn't reply, Vera asked, 'How long were you out there?'

'I'd been at sea about three weeks when I got caught in the storm. How many days after that — I really don't know. Too many.'

'It must have been terrible.'

'It was . . . ' Glen's voice trailed off.

Vera wasn't sure what she could say or do. The man was obviously deeply affected by his close brush with death. She was still searching for the right words, when Glen spoke again.

'Wait a minute. You said Horsley? Vera Horsley?'

Vera recognised the tone of his voice. 'Shh,' she said. 'No one knows.'

'No one knows?' Glen looked amazed. 'How can that be? If I'd had my wits about me, I would have recognised you straight away. I have all . . . I *had* all your books. They are all in Davey Jones' Locker now.'

'I'll send you some new ones when we get back,' Vera said.

'So, tell me, is this a holiday or are you researching your next book? *Murder at the Mizzenmast* or some such?'

'Actually, I was thinking *Buried at Sea*,' Vera said.

'So you're researching here on this ship,' Glen said. 'That's great.'

'Yes, but no one can know, or they'll start being strange when I am around,' Vera said. 'For some reason, the fact that I'm a crime writer bothers people. They think I am probably a bit strange myself if I can think up all those serial killers and such.'

'Your secret is safe with me.' Glen gave her a conspiratorial wink.

'And when . . . if . . . you want to talk about your ordeal,' Vera said, 'you'll find me a good listener. I will even promise not to use it in a book . . . well, not directly.'

He smiled again.

Oh, my, Vera thought. He is most

definitely hero material.

'Vera?'

Speaking of hero material, Vera turned back to the handsome doctor who had just emerged from the examination area.

'I wasn't bothering him, honestly,' she said quickly.

'I know you weren't,' William said, drawing her to one side. 'It's about Lian.'

'How is she? The baby . . . ?'

'The baby's fine,' said the doctor. 'But she tells me she and you have become friends of sorts.'

'Yes. She's a lovely girl.'

'Would you be able to keep a bit of an eye of her for me,' the doctor spoke in a low voice. 'I'm sure she'll be fine, but if I know you are there to help her if she needs it . . . well, I will feel better about her.'

'Of course,' Vera said earnestly.

'Thanks. She can go now, but she needs to rest.'

'I'll see she does.'

'And I'll make sure I don't tell your secret to anyone either,' William winked at her.

'William! You know?'

'Of course I do,' he replied. 'When you started asking me all those questions, you had to be planning a murder or writing about one. I assumed the latter.'

'Ah . . . but are you certain?' Vera tossed her head and waggled her eyebrows. She raised her voice just a little. 'Now, Lian, my dear. Let's go find ourselves a nice cup of tea.'

14

Kit felt like an intruder. Like death hovering on the edges of the masked ball — or in this case leaning on the bar at the back of the observation lounge. Pulling a pen from his pocket, he quickly sketched a death's head on a paper cocktail napkin. He was blacking in the area around the empty eye sockets, when he heard her laugh.

He looked up, searching the crowded room. Jenny was standing near one of the big glass windows. They were so far south now, that darkness was a stranger, and Jenny was framed in the gentle light of a very low sun. She was talking to the elderly lady with the big purple handbag. And standing next to her was the guest of honour. Glen Stewart. The man who had survived that dramatic rescue.

He looked like a man who had been

to the gates of hell and back. His face was gaunt and even from a distance, Kit could see the bruises. People were crowding around him, and Kit could tell from the set of his body, that the man was starting to tire. He was looking around, as if to escape.

Kit knew that feeling well. Some people seemed to feed on the pain of others. Even well-wishers were exhausting when they wouldn't leave you alone. And he was as bad as anyone in the room. He too was only here to look at the man who had come so close to death . . . and fought his way back.

Across the room, Glen turned and their eyes met. For a few seconds, their gaze held, then Kit looked away. The habit of hiding had become ingrained. He picked up his pen again, just to give himself something to do. This time the sketch was a small yacht . . . with a wave towering above it. The wave was shaped like a hand, fingers outstretched like claws trying to grasp the yacht.

'That's actually pretty much what it felt like.'

Kit slowly lifted his eyes from the sketch. Glen was standing beside him, his empty glass in his hand.

'You must be glad it's over,' he said, taking refuge in platitudes.

'I am.' Glen signalled the barman for another glass of water. 'Although I am beginning to think facing this crowd is almost as bad.' Glen smiled to take the sting out of his words. 'I may have to punch the next person who asks me what it felt like out there.'

Kit looked at the man's tired eyes. That's not what he wanted to ask. He wanted to ask what had driven Glen to fight so hard to survive. Was there a wife or a child somewhere waiting for him? Was that what drove him on? Love? How much love did you need to fight that sort of pain? And if the love wasn't strong enough . . .

'This is really good, you know,' Glen said, lifting the sketch from the top of the bar for closer inspection.

225

'Keep it,' Kit said. He turned away. He had to get out of here before someone came looking for Glen — and found him as well.

Kit stepped through the door, letting it shut behind him. The ship was in smooth waters now. Despite the delay to their journey, they would reach the ice tomorrow. All the passengers would go ashore. But not Kit. Tomorrow he must do what he had come to do. He couldn't wait any longer.

★   ★   ★

'Look at this.' Glen appeared at Jenny's side again, holding a white paper napkin out for her inspection.

She froze as she saw the drawing.

'Oh, look.' Vera plucked the napkin from Glen's fingers. 'It's another of those drawings. Is your mystery man here?'

Jenny turned her head towards the bar. 'I can't see him . . . '

'I think he left,' Glen said, retrieving

the napkin. 'You know . . . This is rather good. I think I will keep it as a souvenir.'

'Sorry, I have to go,' Jenny said.

Vera looked at her and raised a single eyebrow.

Glen put his hand on her arm.

'Jenny, it was good to talk to you. You know, I am moving into the crew quarters.'

'Sorry?' Jenny was surprised. 'Into the crew quarters?'

'Yes. I can't stay in sick bay. They might need the bed for someone who is really sick. The passenger cabins are all full. But I was told one of the lecturers didn't come — so their cabin in the crew quarters is free. That's where they are going to put me. So, we'll be neighbours.'

'That's great,' Jenny said automatically. 'If there's anything I can do, let me know. But, sorry, I have to go now.'

Realising that she was being almost rude, Jenny pushed her way through the lounge and out the doors. At the stairs she hesitated. Down one flight was the luxury cabin where her mysterious friend lived. But she knew instinctively that he wouldn't be there. She headed for the top deck.

The wind was icy as she stepped outside. But she was right. There was a solitary figure standing by the railing.

She started toward him, and then stopped. What was she thinking? If he wanted to talk to her, he would have done it at the party. He was obviously a man who enjoyed solitude and here she was behaving like some stalker. Not only that, he was a passenger; and not just any passenger. He had the biggest, most expensive cabin on the ship. And she was just a first time lecturer. She could lose her job over this. Not that they were likely to throw her off the ship mid-ocean. But it still wasn't . . .

'Hello, Jenny.'

'Hello, Kit.'

'This is getting to be a habit.'

'Oh, I am so sorry,' Jenny said,

feeling flustered. 'I didn't mean to intrude.' She started to back away.

'No, please stay.'

He turned to look at her and she could see an indescribable need . . . a hunger in his eyes. But not for her.

'Please.' Kit said again, ever so softly.

'All right.' She stepped up and took a position beside him, her hands on the rail and together they stared out over the ocean.

The twilight was soft and although the ocean looked as cold as it no doubt was, it appeared far less threatening than it had just twenty-four hours earlier.

'There's no sign of our friends, the albatross.' Jenny said.

'With so much of the world to explore, we really can't expect them to stay with us.'

'I guess not. But it was lovely to watch them together like that.'

For a long time Kit remained silent. Jenny was beginning to wonder why, when at last he spoke again.

'Glen seemed to be enjoying the party.'

'I guess after a close call like that, it feels good just to be alive.'

'I imagine it does. I saw the two of you talking. Has he said much about what happened?'

'Not a lot. He got caught up in the storm. He was doing all right until a freak wave smashed his boat.' Jenny stopped talking for a minute, her mind redrawing the image of Glen's face as he'd answered questions about his ordeal. 'He said there were times he thought he was going to die . . . '

'But he kept fighting.'

'Yes, of course he did,' Jenny said. 'Wouldn't you?'

For a very long moment, there was no reply. Jenny felt a strange fear deep inside her. She looked across at the man standing with her at the railing. 'Kit? You would have kept fighting . . . wouldn't you?'

'Of course.'

He didn't meet her eye, and Jenny

230

felt a coldness descend on her that had nothing to do with the weather or the latitude. He was lying.

'His life was on the line,' Jenny said forcefully. 'And he fought for it. You would. I would. Anyone would.'

He turned to face her then. He was very close, looking down at her with an intensity that made his blue eyes seem deeper than the ocean. He gripped her by the shoulders as if he were drowning, and she was his life preserver.

'You would, wouldn't you, Jenny. You would fight. You'd never give up. You'd never leave . . . someone you loved.'

'Never!' The fierceness of her answer surprised her. Yet she meant it. Even more importantly, she wanted Kit to know she meant it, because right now she was afraid for him. More afraid than she had been for Glen even in those moments when he disappeared under the waves. 'I would always keep fighting. Life is too precious to let go of it easily. I would fight for myself. For the people I love . . . and the people who love me.'

His face was just inches from her own — and she quivered with the need to kiss him. It wasn't about love or lust — it was about life. And never giving up.

His eyes searched her face. He lifted one hand to tenderly touch her cheek with the back of one finger. His ran his finger along the fading mark where she had scratched her cheek. The wound had healed, but his touch was so light, so gentle, she could barely feel it. His eyes glistened with tears not brought about by the biting cold and the wind, but rather by some terrible pain she could sense deep inside him.

'You would never give up,' he whispered.

She closed her eyes unable to stand the power of his gaze, and felt his hand drop from her shoulder. When she opened her eyes again, he was leaving, striding quickly away across the freezing, windswept deck. Jenny stood rooted in place as he vanished down the stairs.

'What just happened?' she asked herself in a whisper.

Whatever it was, she couldn't leave it there. She almost broke into a run as she crossed the deck. It took just a moment to descend to deck six, but when she looked along the corridor towards the stern, Kit was not to be seen.

She hesitated. She should not go to his cabin. She should not knock on his door and demand to know why he had looked at her like that. Why he had placed such emphasis on that word. *You* would never give up. *You*. What did that mean? She had to find out.

'Jenny, there you are.' Before she could move, a female voice stopped her in her tracks. It was Anna. She sighed and gave her attention to the nurse, who also happened to be her boss's wife.

'I'm just putting some things together to put in the spare cabin for Glen. You know he's going to be in the staff quarters? He'll be right next to you, so can we rely on you to help him out?'

Anna didn't seem to notice her lack of response.

'I knew we could count on you,' she continued. 'So why don't you come with me now and we can get some stuff squared away for him.'

Without giving her time to answer, Anna started down the stairs and Jenny had no choice but to follow.

15

Kit stood on his private balcony and looked out on an alien world.

It was cold. Far colder than anything he had ever experienced. A strong wind added an extra cutting edge to the chill in the air. The grey sea moved restlessly, tossed and twisted by the wind, but compared to the storm, it was nothing to the cruise ship. The deck was solid and stable beneath Kit's feet, but that gave no feeling of safety.

The ocean was full of ice. Blue ice. White ice.

Huge icebergs drifted in the grey deep. Some were like vast plateaus — flat topped with sheer sides that fell straight to the water. Others were jagged, and sharp. Carved by wind and water into fantastic shapes. Here was a berg with the centre completely eroded away. A medium sized boat could sail through that icy arch, if its commander was foolish enough.

Smaller chunks of ice bobbed in the waters, tossed by the waves and the ship's wake. The sound of the *Cape Adare*'s steel hull scraping though the ice was almost a cry of pain. Movement in the distance drew Kit's eye. The side of an iceberg was collapsing. Huge chunks of ice slid into the sea, causing a surge of ice-filled water. The sudden shift in the berg's balance caused it to begin a slow roll, its underside rising out of the water as it toppled onto a new plane.

Icebergs such as this had claimed the mighty Titanic. What chance did the tiny *Cape Adare* stand in the face of the powerful and treacherous forces that ruled these frozen wastes?

The ship was changing course, turning slowly and as it swung, something began to emerge through the haze. Something that was not ice.

Dark grey cliffs rose out of the ocean, towering above their vessel. This would be Cape Adare, the ship's namesake and their first stop on the vast white wilderness of Antarctica. Kit stood for a while, watching the grey cliffs draw ever closer. They seemed more solid than the ice — but equally as threatening.

The cruise itinerary had listed Cape Adare as a place to go ashore, but all landings were dependant on the weather. The only way to land would be in rubber boats. Surely not today, Kit thought. Surely they wouldn't take a small boat out in that treacherous sea, where the ice seemed to be waiting to crush anything that invaded its territory. The waves were growing less violent as they moved closer to the shelter of the cape, but Kit still didn't believe they would attempt a landing.

Until he realised the ship was slowing down.

Until he heard the sound of the anchor chain dropping and realised that soon the crew would be loading passengers onto those small boats and setting them down in the perilous seas.

Signing on for this cruise hadn't been about playing tourist. Kit had other reasons for being on board. But as he stood looking out over the shifting ocean of ice, he knew he was about to do something very foolish.

Because Jenny was going to be on board one of those small boats. The tender lobby, from where the small boats were loaded, was semi-controlled chaos.

Encased in two thick jumpers, her heavy jacket and a life jacket as well as fur-lined gum boots and a thick woolly hat, Jenny felt like she could barely move. Her hands were the only part of her body to retain any usefulness — and that was only because she was wearing just one set of gloves. When the heavy oilskin gloves went over the top of her light woollen ones, her hands would be pretty useless too.

As she moved across the deck, in her mind she imagined the ungainly waddle of a penguin. Jenny the Penguin. That was her. But that was a far better option than frostbite.

'Hi, Jenny,' a male voice at her side caused her to turn.

'Hello, Glen,' she said, quite genuinely pleased to see him. 'What are you doing down here? You're not planning to go on this excursion?'

'I sure am. You know what they say — get back on the horse as soon as you fall off it.'

Jenny looked at him closely. The bruises and cuts on his body hadn't fully healed yet, but his eyes had lost that haunted tiredness she had seen at the party.

'Have you moved into the new quarters yet?' Jenny asked. 'I'm sorry, I was going to help but I've been busy getting everything ready for this excursion . . . '

'I got the key this morning. There was nothing to move . . . as I have nothing,' he shrugged, but there was sadness in it. 'There were some things in my cabin. Clothes. A razor. That sort of thing. I'm told I have you to thank for that.'

'Not really,' she said. 'Anna got everything together for you. I just helped.'

'Well, thank you anyway.'

Jenny decided he would have a really nice smile when the last of the bruises faded. She couldn't help but smile back at him. As she did, her eyes flashed to the stairway. A pair of legs appeared, followed by the same heavy-duty jacket that everyone else was wearing. But there was nothing commonplace about the face that followed it.

Kit was here!

Her first thought was why? He had seemed so determined to avoid the company of the other passengers and the crew. The only time he had so far appeared in public was those few minutes at the back of the party — when all eyes were on Greg and Kit could pass unnoticed. Why was he now walking towards her through the tumult of boarding the passengers onto the boats? She hadn't pegged him as the sort of person who was up for sightseeing.

'Jenny!' A strong masculine voice that belonged to neither of the men she was thinking about caused Jenny to turn.

'This is your boat,' Karl Anders said as he waved her forward.

'Yes, boss,' she said.

The Zodiac was bobbing gently in the lee of the ship, just below the open hatch. The big outboard engine was idling, under the control of a seaman wearing as much protective clothing as Jenny. A small part of his face was visible through the layers of fur and Jenny recognised the same seaman who had first brought her to the *Adare* back in Sydney . . . when freezing to death had seemed such an unlikely event.

Slipping her last layer of protection onto her hands, Jenny walked to the hatch and lightly stepped down into the Zodiac. Seaman Brown waved her to her position at the front. Jenny lowered herself onto the rubber side of the boat, gripping rope lines with both hands. She hadn't liked her last ride with Seaman Brown, and she was beginning to think this one was going to be equally scary. To distract herself, she began to think about the lecture she was going to have to give when they reached land. Penguins, she told herself. Lots and lots about penguins.

The boat leaped suddenly as the first passenger added his weight to the load.

'Here we go,' Glen said as he took a place right next to Jenny. His head twisted swiftly as he looked around, and Jenny caught what she thought might have been a flash of fear in his eyes. That wasn't surprising, given his recent brush with a watery grave.

Jenny shuddered as another passenger sat down on her other side. She didn't have to look to know who this was and she wondered if that feeling of someone waltzing on her grave was brought about by Glen's presence . . . or Kit's.

The two men exchanged nods, but didn't speak.

'Well, isn't this just so exciting?'

Of course, Vera would be on her boat. It was fate really. It was also the first time Jenny had seen the older woman without her giant purple handbag. Where, Jenny wondered, was the ever-present notebook? Vera would still have it on her, Jenny was sure.

'Is Lian with you?' Jenny asked as Vera settled herself close to Glen.

'No, dear. She's not feeling up to an excursion. But this is going to be an adventure, isn't it?'

Vera directed the question at all those around her, including the other passengers who were taking their seats. Several of the English students Jenny had met earlier were on board the boat. Without their chaperone. Jenny guessed that made her the responsible adult. Jenny was inclined to agree with Vera. This was going to be exciting, although, she thought as she cast quick sideways glances at both Kit and Glen, just what kind of excitement, she really wasn't sure.

'Hello,' Vera said, holding out one hand toward Kit. 'I'm Vera. And you are . . . ?'

'Christopher. Kit.' The second was said hesitantly, as if he was afraid of letting Vera get too close.

'Hello, Kit,' Vera continued, totally unabashed. 'I am so excited about this excursion. You know Scott's team wintered here. They all died later, of course. They must have suffered terribly during that final march across the ice . . . '

A shout from the hatchway above signalled their departure. The slow but powerful surge of the big outboard engine pushed the Zodiac away from the ship's hull towards the stark headland. Here at sea level, the sound of ice scraping on ice was loud. Between that and the roar of the outboard engine, Jenny didn't bother trying to talk to her passengers. The boat was being tossed about by the sea, and she noticed Vera slide closer to Glen. Jenny too was holding on with both hands with all her strength. Her sprained wrist was no longer bandaged, and the doctor had declared her fit to take this outing. But occasionally as the boat jarred, she felt just a slight twinge of pain. She was very conscious of Kit's silent form beside her. She turned and looked up at him. His face was expressionless as he stared out over the icy water. What was he thinking, she wondered?

A powerful thump as the boat crashed down off a wave caused her heart to skip a beat. She was beginning to not like this at all. She turned towards Seaman Brown. He caught her eye and slowly shook his head. Relief surged through her. The boat began to turn back towards the ship. The penguins would pass this day undisturbed.

'I'm sorry,' Jenny yelled to the passengers. 'It's too rough. We won't be able to land. We'll head back to the ship now.'

She saw a mixture of relief and disappointment on the faces in front of her. Slowly she looked sideways at Kit. But his face was still without expression. She had the feeling that his mind was a long way from their little boat and its struggles in the icy sea. She would love to know where.

Karl and some crew members were waiting at the boat hatch to help the passengers from the boat. As part of the expedition team, Jenny was the second last to leave. Seaman Brown remained on board to shepherd the Zodiac up the side of the ship and back to its place on the deck. Jenny remembered the time she had ridden the boat up the ship's side. She was very glad to step onto — if not dry land — then at least the firm deck. When she looked around, Vera and Glen were waiting for her. As was her boss. But Kit was gone.

'I've directed the passengers into the lecture theatre,' Karl said. 'As soon as they have removed a few layers of

246

clothing. You should meet them there and we'll do the *Adare* lecture.'

Jenny nodded. For each location on their cruise, there was a lecture and slide show as standby for days like these — when weather prevented a landing. 'Sure,' she said.

'Let's keep each other company on the way,' Glen said. 'After all, we're neighbours now.'

There was nothing wrong with the way he said it. And there was no reason they shouldn't walk together. It wasn't as if . . . anyone . . . would see them together and get the wrong idea.

'Perhaps I should go with Vera,' she said turning to the older woman. 'In case you need some help.'

'No. No,' Vera waved off the suggestion with a meaningful look. 'You two young people go along. I might just stop by the sick bay and see if William is there.'

There was no way out without seeming rude, and Jenny didn't want to do that. She also didn't want to give Glen, or Vera for that matter, any encouragement. She cast about hopelessly for an answer, and then gave in.

'Let's go,' she said to Glen. 'But we should hurry. I need to prep the lecture.'

The locked door to the crew quarters was on the other side of the tender lobby, behind the lifts. Jenny quickly punched in the security code. The hallway leading towards the front of the ship was empty. Jenny moved swiftly towards her door. Glen stopped next to her.

As she slipped her key card into the lock, Jenny was acutely aware of Glen waiting. Not moving to open his own door. She realised that maybe Glen was already getting ideas of his own.

'I'll be a few minutes,' she said cheerfully. 'I have to get my lecture notes and things. So you should go on ahead of me. Make sure you get a good seat.'

'All right. I'll see you there.'

If he was disappointed, he didn't

show it. Maybe she was the one getting the wrong idea . . . or maybe he was just a patient man.

16

Even at three a.m. there was enough light for Kit to see the image he had created on the paper napkin. To see her eyes looking back at him. He had drawn her long auburn hair loose around her face. And her lips were smiling.

But something was wrong.

Those were not his wife's eyes.

Kit lifted his face to stare out over the ocean. The sun was low on the horizon and the light had a soft pink tinge to it. During the night they had passed into the Ross Sea — and the water was calm and glassy, although still dotted with ice. He closed his eyes and tried to picture her face — the face he had loved for a decade or more. But he just couldn't do it.

He opened his eyes and reached for another bar napkin. Somewhere deep inside him, in the place that was the core of his being, he found what he was searching for. The pen in his hand moved quickly and with assurance across the soft white paper.

This time — the face that looked back at him was the right one.

He laid the two napkins side by side . . . and wondered . . .

The lounge door opened with a loud crash.

Startled, Kit turned his head to see what looked like a tree falling through the doorway. Quickly he slipped the sketch — the right one — into the safety of his pocket.

'Oh. Sir. I'm sorry. I didn't expect there to be anyone in the lounge this late . . . umm . . . early.' The crewman looked flustered. 'I've got to put this up, you see, sir. Now we're here.'

Kit could now see that 'this' was indeed a tree. A Christmas tree. How could he have forgotten the date?

'It was too rough before, sir,' the crewman continued. 'But now . . . well I have the captain's orders.'

'Of course,' Kit said. 'Go right ahead. I was just leaving.'

'There's no need to leave, sir,' the seaman added. 'I'll just be here in the corner with the tree. There are some decorations to go up as well.'

Even more of a reason for him to leave. There were too many memories that would come rushing back if he allowed them to. Christmas with Dana. Christmas without her. Kit stood up and moved rapidly towards the door. He turned towards the stairs that would lead to the top of the ship and the place he had spent so many hours staring out to sea. The place he had waited. The place where Jenny would join him.

He changed direction in mid-stride and almost ran down the long corridor towards his stateroom. Once the door closed behind him, he pulled the napkin from his pocket. Gently he spread it on the table. He stood looking down at his drawing for a few moments. The boxes he had so far failed to open were all stacked in the corner behind the table. He turned to them now and began tearing them open in a kind of frenzy.

He found the huge sheet of oilskin and carried it to the glass doors that led to his balcony. It would be cold out there. Too cold. He glanced around his beautifully appointed stateroom and shrugged. He could always offer to buy new carpet. Once the oilskin was down, he set up the rest of his tools.

He paused then to look at the bar napkin again. He pulled out the sketches he had done during the voyage so far and spread those out on the table. A couple fell to the floor but he left them there.

He was close. He was so close. But had he come far enough? The passion and inspiration that had deserted him . . . was it back?

Silence echoed through the room. Silence echoed through his heart and soul.

Frustration began to claim him again, but this time he was determined the anger and the darkness would not win. He shook his head, and his gaze fell on the small cabinet beside his bed. He strode over and pulled open the top drawer. The drawer was empty except for a small white envelope. He lifted it, feeling the weight of something not made of paper. He tried not to look at the printing on the envelope. The text and logo were in sombre colours that suited people who dealt with death. The envelope was shabby. It had travelled far. He turned to look at the seal, closed a lifetime ago. Then he tore the top and tipped the contents into his hand.

The gold shone dully. The diamond sparkled even in the dim light streaming through the glass doors leading to the balcony. He closed his hand around the ring and the memories came flooding back. That day in the park. Dana so beautiful. The tears in her eyes as he slipped this ring on her finger. It was the happiest day of his life with other even happier days to follow. Until the darkness came to claim them both.

Fingers still clenched around the ring, Kit opened the sliding glass doors and walked out onto his balcony. It was freezing. The wind had dropped and the ocean was still — but it was so cold that it was painful on the bare skin of his face and fingers.

The ship lay at anchor. The water was like a mirror. He opened his fingers and looked at the ring one more time.

'Goodbye, Dana,' he whispered, conscious of the tears streaming down his cheeks. Were they caused by the wind? Or by what he was about to do? He didn't know. He didn't care. There was no one to see him. To blame him. No one but himself.

He stepped to the railing, and closed his fist once more around the ring. He took a deep breath and threw the ring as far as he could. His eyes lost it. He caught no glimpse of gold. No flash of light reflected from the diamond. Not even a ripple where it fell.

But it was gone.

He didn't give himself time to think.

He turned back to his cabin, leaving the doors open so the pain of that freezing wind would stay with him. He looked at the tools laid out on the table. He pictured a smiling face and short dark hair. He heard her laugh. And talk to the dolphins. He reached for the brightest colours.

⋆　⋆　⋆

The tree was lovely. It wasn't a real tree, of course. But it was beautiful anyway. Red and gold tinsel glistened in the light from what seemed like a hundred tiny silver bulbs. There were gleaming round balls of the same colours. And candy canes. And right at the top of the tree, a star shone brightly, lit from within.

Lian thought it was the most beautiful tree she had ever seen. Her parents had migrated to Australia as newly-wed adults and had never really adopted the western Christmas traditions. They celebrated the Lunar New

Year and Tomb Sweeping Day. The Ghost festival rated highly in her family. But not Christmas. Lian had always loved the traditional Chinese celebrations, but she was as Australian as she was Chinese. Her parents had never really understood how much she wanted a family Christmas as well. She had joined school friends and work colleagues for Christmas parties, but that just wasn't the same. Spending Christmas on board ship with her new friends would, in some ways, be easier than spending the holiday in her parents' home.

'You will be so lucky, little one,' she said softly. 'You will get both traditions. You'll have the hungry ghosts and Santa Claus. I promise.' She wasn't in much of a position to make promises, but she knew that this one she would keep.

She made her way towards a table by the side window. From there she had a glorious view out over the ice-studded ocean. She wouldn't be taking any excursions. She wasn't about to risk her baby by venturing into a tiny rubber boat. In some ways, the thought saddened her. She would have liked to see something of this amazing place. After all, Colin lived and worked here . . . and would until after their baby was born. Lian closed her eyes and forced back a tear. It was going to be all right. It really was. It had to be . . .

'Lian, you're up and about early.' Vera settled herself into a chair.

'I couldn't sleep.'

'Is everything all right. You're feeling fine?'

'Yes. Just nervous. Tomorrow we should be at McMurdo Station.'

Vera beamed. 'I imagine you're anxious to see your young man. And he no doubt feels the same.'

'He doesn't know I'm coming,' Lian whispered.

'Doesn't know?' Vera's carefully arched eyebrows shot up. 'But surely you have let him know you're on the ship?'

Lian shook her head. 'We e-mail

every day. But I haven't told him.'

'Why ever not?' Vera asked.

'He'd want to know why I was coming and then I'd have to tell him about the baby. I wanted to do that in person.'

'Oh, my dear.'

Vera reached out to pat her hand in a motherly fashion, something that Lian found rather comforting. Her own mother wasn't one for casual outward displays of affection.

'You have to tell him. Today,' Vera said. 'He has to know you are coming — otherwise he might be away from the base on some expedition. You might miss him altogether.'

Lian's heart sank. She hadn't even thought of that. She buried her face in her hands. Everything she touched was turning bad.

'Now. Don't you worry,' Vera said. 'Let's just go down to the internet café. There won't be anyone there at this hour. You can e-mail him. You don't have to tell him about the baby. You could say it is a Christmas surprise.'

Lian thought about that for a few seconds. 'That's a really good idea, Vera,' she said. 'I don't know why I didn't think of that.'

'I've had a bit more practice,' said Vera getting to her feet. As she did, something caught her eye. She leaned over to retrieve a white bar napkin from the floor.

'Oh . . . ' said Vera.

Intrigued, Lian leaned over for a closer look.

'It's another one of those drawings.'

Vera spread it out on the table. The sketch was of a woman, smiling out at them. She was quite beautiful, with long hair curling down to her shoulders.

'I know this is silly,' Lian said, 'but I think she looks a little bit like Jenny.'

'That's not silly,' Vera said. 'It's the eyes. She has Jenny's eyes. Isn't that interesting?'

Vera tucked the sketch into her handbag and together they left the lounge. At deck five, they parted ways. While Vera returned to her own cabin, Lian headed down one more flight of stairs. The internet café was deserted, but the PCs were sitting there, their screens glowing dully. Lian lowered herself into a chair and wiggled a mouse. The screen in front of her sprang to life, inviting her to take advantage of the free internet service the ship was pleased to offers its guests.

Quickly she logged in to her e-mail. There was nothing new waiting for her. Colin had e-mailed yesterday — but she'd already read that one. More than once.

New e-mail.

Hi Colin, she wrote. *I've got a surprise for you — I hope you'll think it's a good one.*

17

The two men were standing at either side of the tender lobby — and Vera had a pretty good idea they were both waiting for the same person.

She stopped by the corner of the lift, pretty much hidden from view, and watched both of them. They were so very different.

Glen was talking to the people around him. No doubt they were still asking about the dramatic rescue, but that didn't seem to bother him. His bruises were fading and it was becoming increasingly obvious that he really was a handsome man, with his sandy hair and blue eyes. In fact, Vera suddenly realised, quite a few of the people talking to him were women. That made sense.

Kit, on the other hand was standing alone. His stiff body language discouraged casual conversation. His brooding good looks attracted covert glances from the women, but no one approached him. None of the women seemed willing to look past that cold outer shell. No — there was one.

Jenny was standing by the door that led to the crew quarters and she too was watching Glen and Kit. She was frowning slightly, but as her eyes rested on Kit, the frown was replaced by an entirely different look. Then she stepped into the boat lobby. At almost the exact some moment, both men turned to look at her. Glen smiled broadly. Kit didn't, but something in his eyes changed.

'Oh,' thought Vera. 'So that's how it is.'

She wasn't really surprised. Jenny was a lovely girl. Attractive and fun. She positively glowed with life and energy. Any man with a pulse would notice her, particularly on a ship where there were few single women. And most of those were, like Vera, no longer in their prime.

As for the men . . . both were

extremely attractive. In different ways.

Vera looked from one man to the other. Then back to Jenny. The girl might not be aware of it, but her face told Vera everything she needed to know.

'I'd better do something about that,' Vera muttered under her breath.

'Today's expedition is to Cape Hallett,' Karl Anders' voice boomed out across the crowded lobby. 'As yesterday's landing was cancelled due to the weather, today we are visiting another penguin rookery. The Adélie penguins here were pushed away by earlier explorers wanting to build a station. But that station has been abandoned, and so the penguins are back.'

Vera saw Karl wave Jenny forward.

'Let's start loading the boats,' the big man continued. 'Jenny will take the first Zodiac.'

At that announcement, both Glen and Kit moved forward to be at the front of the queue for Jenny's boat. If Vera was going to make a move, now was the time. Jenny was still making her way through the crowd. Vera stepped forward until she was in her path. As her friend approached, Vera suddenly gave a little cry and staggered.

'Vera!' Jenny was at her side in a heartbeat. 'Are you all right?'

'I'm feeling a little faint, Jenny,' Vera whispered.

'Don't worry. I'll help you back to your cabin,' Jenny's voice, full of genuine concern, gave Vera just a twinge of guilt.

'Thank you,' she said, struggling to keep her voice quivering.

Jenny put an arm around Vera's shoulders and somehow managed to catch her boss's eye through the crowd surging towards the boat hatch.

Karl nodded and Jenny began to guide Vera towards the lifts.

While they waited for the lift to arrive, Vera risked a quick glance across at the boat hatch. Glen was gone, already loaded into the Zodiac. Kit was standing by the open hatch, obviously torn. He had wanted to go with Jenny, but to decline to step into the boat now would have attracted too much of the attention that he hated. A second later, he turned towards the Zodiac and was gone.

Vera felt a surge of energy. Yes! She struggled to remain bowed over, as if with tiredness until the lift arrived and she and Jenny were alone inside it.

'Right,' she said straightening her back. 'First we need to stop at deck three.'

'But Vera, your cabin is on five.' Jenny's voice had taken on the soothing tone of a nurse.

'I know that, Jenny,' Vera said. 'But that's not where we are going.'

'We're not?'

'No. We're not.'

At that moment the doors opened and Vera led the way out into the main reception area. Now they were fully underway, the area was deserted. Vera moved swiftly to the desk and the computer on it.

'Vera, what's going on?' Jenny asked. 'I thought you were ill.'

'I'm fine, my dear,' Vera said, quickly glancing around the desk. She reached for the top draw, but it was locked.

'Damn,' she muttered under her breath

'Vera!' Jenny's voice was stern. 'What's going on?'

'We don't have a lot of time,' Vera said. 'Have you got your cabin key-card on you?'

'Of course,' Jenny said.

'Can I have it for a moment?'

Jenny dug into the pocket of her jacket and handed it over. Vera examined it closely.

'I thought as much,' she said. 'The crew cards are different. This should work then.'

She slid the card into the slot on the card reader next to the registration desk computer. The she reached for the keyboard.

'Vera!' Jenny exclaimed.

'Shhh! Keep your voice down. I'm

trying to concentrate.'

Vera studied the screen and reached for the mouse. A couple of clicks put her exactly where she wanted to be. There was the name Mr Christopher Walker. And the cabin number 642.

'What are you doing?' Jenny whispered, looking frantically around in case someone else was watching.

'Reprogramming your cabin key.'

'What! Why?'

'We need to investigate something.'

'Investigate what?'

Vera didn't bother answering. Her task completed, she retrieved Jenny's card from the reader and set off towards the lift. Jenny followed.

'How did you learn to do that?' Jenny asked as the doors slid shut on them.

'Just something I learned. You pick up all sorts of strange things in my line of work,' Vera answered.

'Your line . . . ' Jenny's voice trailed off.

Ah, thought Vera. At last.

'Vera Horsley . . . What's your middle

name?' Jenny asked slowly.

'Josephine.'

'V.J. Horsley. There's a crime writer by that name.'

'Yes there is,' Vera admitted.

'That's you!'

'Yes. Now come on.' The lift doors opened and Vera led the way down a long corridor. Jenny followed, her frown deepening as she absorbed the information she had just received. It wasn't until Vera stopped outside a door that Jenny seemed to return to the present. She looked at the name of the suite and turned to Vera, her face a mask of shock.

'No! Vera. You can't just break into someone's cabin.'

'It's not breaking. I have a key.' Vera slipped the card into the slot.

'No!' Jenny grabbed hold of her arm. Vera winced at the force with which the girl was holding her. 'I'll get fired.'

'No you won't. I'm a crime writer. I know how to cover our tracks.' Vera pushed the door open a crack. 'He's hiding something. Aren't you just a little bit curious?'

Jenny's hesitation was all the answer she needed to give. Vera pushed against the heavy cabin door with all her strength. It slowly opened and both women stepped across the threshold.

Vera let go of the door, oblivious to the sound of it slamming closed. Her jaw dropped as she gazed around the room.

'Oh,' she said. 'He's THAT Kit Walker!'

★   ★   ★

The room was a blaze of colour. A riot that almost overwhelmed her senses. Jenny blinked, her mind staggering as it tried to understand what she was seeing. Canvasses lined the walls. Some were barely started. Others looked complete. Or very nearly so. They were good. They were powerful.

They took her breath away.

Slowly Jenny stepped forward for a

closer look at the painting nearest to her. It showed a sky, shot through with colour. In the sky two giant birds soared together, seeming almost to move through the brilliance around them. Albatross, paired in flight. As she looked at them, Jenny had a feeling as if there was someone else in that painting. Someone just out of sight. Someone reflected in the shadows of the birds eyes. Someone who could be . . .

She shook her head and moved to the next painting. Dolphins danced on the waves, life and joy and light seeming to shine from them as they played. Their bodies were half twisted in the air as if to look back at someone. Someone just outside the frame of the painting. Someone who was watching them.

It couldn't be her. Could it?

The painting of the ice was as blinding in its intensity as the ice itself had been yesterday. Not white, but all the colours of the rainbow flashing through the painting as she moved towards it. And at one side, a wisp of something that might be the watcher's dark hair.

'Jenny.' Vera's soft voice drew her attention to a painting propped on a chair.

This one was far from complete, but already the image was leaping from the canvas. A girl on the deck of a boat. Looking out over the ocean. Her face was turned slightly away from the painter, but it was clear from the toss of her head that she was laughing. Jenny could almost hear the sound. Even incomplete, it was a breathtaking piece of art. It was . . .

'Me?' Jenny said.

'Yes. You.' Vera's voice was full of awe.

'I don't understand,' Jenny said, struggling to get the words out.

'You really don't know who he is, do you?' Vera said.

Jenny shook her head. 'I didn't take art at school, and at uni I was always too busy studying . . . ' And falling in love with a professor, she added to herself. An arrogant underhand cheat of a man, who didn't deserve to be mentioned in the same breath as the artist who had produced the paintings that lined the cabin.

'Kit Walker was . . . is . . . a brilliant artist who took the world by storm. He's Australian, but his work soon took him to New York and London. He was feted as a genius. He married a principle dancer from the New York ballet . . . '

Jenny felt her heart clench at those words. 'Married . . . ?'

'Yes,' Vera continued. 'She was so beautiful. I saw her dance once. She was like an angel. It was a fairy tale. The artist and the dancer. Until it ended in tragedy.'

Jenny dragged her eyes away from the painting and looked at Vera. The older woman was visibly moved by the story she was telling. And by the great passion in the paintings that surrounded them.

'What happened?'

Vera took a slow deep breath. 'No one knows for sure. There was a lot of speculation in the media. Some people said it was suicide. Some said he killed her.'

'No!' The exclamation was out before Jenny could stop it. 'He wouldn't. He couldn't . . . '

An image sprang unbidden to her mind. Kit on the top deck in the darkness. His face inches from her own. His words echoed softly in her mind . . . *You would, wouldn't you, Jenny. You would fight. You'd never give up. You'd never leave . . . someone you loved.*

'He vanished from public view then,' Vera continued. 'They said he'd stopped painting. The work he'd already done became even more valuable. Some of the tabloids suggested he had killed himself in grief at losing her.'

Jenny's mind flashed back to those first nights on the cruise. Kit standing on the upper deck staring out to sea. Was that why he had come to this wild place? Had he been planning to kill himself? To step off the safety of the deck into the cold dark water? No! She would never believe that.

'But now, it seems he is working again,' Vera said, her voice tinged with awe. 'He's found a new muse.'

Jenny dragged her eyes away from the painting and found Vera looking at her with a strange intensity.

'A new muse . . . '

'You, Jenny. You're his muse now.'

'No.' Jenny almost staggered across the room to perch on the edge of the bed. She gazed around the cabin in confusion. Without thinking she bent to pick up a piece of paper from the floor. It was an old envelope, torn open. She looked at the funeral home logo on the corner and slowly realised that every word Vera had spoken was true. There was no denying any of it. In her heart she knew it was her in those paintings. Or rather, not in them. The thought was almost too much to bear. To be the centre of such passion. Such talent.

Such amazing art. It was a responsibility she didn't want.

The envelope slipped through her fingers back onto the floor.

'Let's go.' Rising to her feet, she took a step and suddenly the desire to get out of this room was overwhelming. She raced to the door and pulled it open. Heedless of whether Vera was following, Jenny raced along the corridor, her feet making a dull thud on the carpet. She turned at the stairway and raced up to the top deck.

It was empty. Jenny moved to the familiar spot where she had stood so often before — sometimes with Kit by her side. She looked out over the water towards the land. She could see a small boat moving back towards the ship.

Was Kit on board that boat, she wondered? Would he be looking for her? Would she be on his mind when he returned to his cabin to take up his brushes again?

Jenny struggled to cope with conflicting emotions. To inspire such work was an honour. To bring some sort of inspiration to a man like Kit was . . . beyond her wildest dreams. To be the subject of such exceptional work was . . . overwhelming.

How was she going to face him again . . . knowing what she now knew?

What was she going to say to him next time they stood together up here, sharing the silence of the night?

18

'Ladies and gentlemen, welcome to McMurdo Station. This is the largest settlement in Antarctica. The one and only Ice-burg!'

A smattering of laughter greeted the expedition leader's comment. Karl's laugh was the loudest of all.

Standing in the lounge, Lian was almost quivering with impatience and nervousness. The *Cape Adare* was gliding gracefully across the ice-filled water, approaching a grey rocky stretch of land that boasted a cluster of buildings and a few roads. Ice and snow covered large parts of the exposed ground. The buildings looked serviceable and solid, but gave no concession to beauty. The overall appearance was bleak and forbidding.

Colin was out there. Waiting for her. He'd responded to her e-mail yesterday, sounding surprised and thrilled at the prospect . . . but also curious. Why, he'd asked, had she taken the trip when they needed to save all their money?

She hadn't replied to that e-mail. She would tell him face to face when they met.

She tugged at the front of the huge jacket she was wearing. Colin hadn't seen her for weeks. How she wished she could be wearing something feminine and sexy when she saw him. But if she tried to go ashore wearing something else, the expedition team would stop her and demand she rugged up for her own good. Still, the jacket negated any possibility Colin might notice a change in her figure. She didn't have a baby bump yet, but she felt different. That was a sure sign that she probably looked different too.

'The ice pier sounds interesting. I wonder if it has ever cracked or broken.' Vera was listening intently to the instructions they were being given for their day ashore. As always, she was taking notes.

There were, apparently, tourist attractions in Antarctica. Shops even. But Lian wasn't interested in any of that. The ship had slowed and was now manoeuvring slowly towards the pier. She strained her eyes forward to see small figures moving around on the ice. Colin was out there. Would he be happy to hear her news? Or would he . . .

'Lian . . . it's going to be all right,' Vera said, patting her arm.

'I know,' Lian replied with a confidence she really didn't feel.

A few minutes later, they both joined the crowd of passengers surging towards the gangway.

'Ladies, please use your room keys to check out,' a crew member instructed them. 'Just place the key against the reader here. That enters your departure in the log. Make sure you do the same thing when you get back on board. We don't want to leave anyone behind.'

'I should hope not,' Vera said.

Lian saw him as soon as she set foot on the gangway. He was standing on the pier, his eyes glued to the hatch. His face was almost hidden by the upturned collar of his jacket, but as his eyes found hers Lian saw a huge smile spread across his face.

She walked carefully down the gangway and fell into his arms. Colin enveloped her in a bear hug. It felt like coming home. She lifted her face to his and kissed him with all the pent up longing of their weeks apart.

It took a few moments before the wolf whistles from those around them seeped into her consciousness.

She pulled back and looked around at the sea of wide grins — many on the faces of people she had never seen before.

'You look so good — even when you are blushing,' Colin said. 'I've missed you so much.'

He ran his fingers down her cheek, prompting another outbreak of whistles.

'Who cares about them,' Colin declared and kissed her again.

Lian wasn't sure whether to laugh or cry. She told herself that it was just hormones when tears began to stream down her cheeks.

'Lian. Honey?' Colin's face creased with concern. 'Is something wrong? Is it your parents? Has something happened?'

'No. My parents think I'm on holiday with friends on the Gold Coast,' Lian said. 'I hated lying to them, but what else could I do?'

'I know.' Colin wrapped his arm around her shoulders and began to lead her away from the crowds. 'I wish you'd let us just tell them. They'll understand. I'm sure they will. They are good people and they love you. And I'm totally lovable too . . . '

He grinned at her, trying to lift her mood. She had to agree with him. He was totally lovable . . . and she loved him with every fibre of her being.

'Is there somewhere we can go

— just to talk? Somewhere private?'
'Sure.'

Colin led her away from the crowded pier. The sun was shining. It wasn't hot, but it wasn't as cold as Lian might have expected. They followed a path away from the town, up a long sloping ridge. At the top they sat on a large rock, with a glorious view over McMurdo. There was open water and ice. The *Cape Adare* sat serenely at rest. Lian could make out the tiny shapes of her fellow passengers as they explored the highlights of possibly the most remote town on the planet. To Lian, it seemed like she was in some sort of a dream. She could only hope it didn't become a nightmare.

'Honey. What is it?' Colin asked gently, taking her hands.

'I'm pregnant.' She didn't dare look at him as she spoke the words. She heard his sharp intake of breath. When he said nothing, she slowly turned to look at him.

His lips were spread in a smile that

almost split his face in half. His brown eyes were shining. There was even the smallest suggestion of a tear in their depths.

'A baby?' Colin said, his voice soft with emotion. 'Really? A baby?'

'Yes.'

'Wow. That's . . . That's . . . Wow.' He leaped to his feet and dragged her off the rock. He flung his arms around her waist and lifted her into the air.

'A baby. We're having a BABY!'

He spun them both around then let her slide back to earth.

'Oh, God. Is that Ok?' he said suddenly. He reached out tentatively to place a hand on her stomach. 'I mean, lifting you like that. It doesn't hurt you or . . . the baby?'

'It's fine. We're fine.' Lian felt the weight of the world begin to lift from her shoulders.

'Wow. When? How? A baby!' The last words were a shout that was carried away by the wind.

The tears streamed down Lian's face.

'I was so afraid,' she said.

'Afraid of what?'

'That you would be angry. That you wouldn't want . . . '

'No. Don't think of that for an instant. Of course I want the baby. Our baby. It's wonderful.' Colin took her face in his hands and kissed away the tears. 'It's earlier than maybe we would have planned. But it's wonderful. I love you. I love our baby. I couldn't be happier.'

He paused, suddenly sobered.

'Lian, you're happy about this too, aren't you?' he asked.

'Of course,' she said. 'It's just . . . well . . . telling my parents is going to be hard.'

'And I'm all the way down here,' Colin added. 'Don't worry. I can come home early. I'll forget wintering on the ice and come home after the summer. I don't want to be apart from you now. We'll find a way to make the money work. It will take me a few weeks before I can get away from here. Can you hold off telling them until I get home?'

'I'll try,' Lian said. 'I really will. It's going to be tough enough telling them that you're not Chinese. But to be pregnant and not married . . . '

Colin raised a finger to her lips to stop her talking.

'We will deal with whatever happens. Together,' he said. 'And as for the not being married bit . . . I think I may have an answer.'

'What do you mean?'

'Lian — this isn't what I planned. How I planned it. But I always knew we would be married one day. You will marry me, won't you?' He suddenly looked uncertain.

Like any young girl, Lian had spent hours imagining this moment. The Proposal. It always had a capital P. In her imagination it had involved a handsome man down on one knee. Champagne. Roses. A ring with a big sparkly diamond. All the things needed to make a perfect moment.

She looked at Colin standing on the

muddy ground and knew she had everything she would ever need or want. 'Of course I will . . . but . . . '

Colin took her hand. 'No buts. I have a plan. Come on.'

★ ★ ★

Jenny was gasping for air as she opened the door to the hut and ducked inside.

'I've got it,' she panted.

Lian and Vera looked at her expectantly as she pulled the rucksack from her back and placed it on the table.

'You'd better open it,' Jenny said as she collapsed into a chair. It had been a long sprint to the ship and back. But they didn't have a lot of time. The *Cape Adare* was only scheduled to be at McMurdo for a few hours. Half that time had already passed when Lian had come to her with the startling news that she was about to get married.

Lian pulled something pale and soft from the rucksack. She grappled with it for a few seconds, then, finding the shoulder seams, held it up.

'Jenny, this is lovely,' she said quietly.

'It's not exactly a wedding dress,' Jenny said, finally beginning to catch her breath. 'But I couldn't let you get married wearing jeans, could I?'

Tears glinted in Lian's eyes. 'It never occurred to me to bring a wedding dress. I was so busy worrying about the baby. And how Colin was going to react. I wanted so much for us to be together, but deep down inside I was afraid it wouldn't happen.'

'It's what you want, dear, isn't it?' Vera asked.

'Oh, yes. More than anything in the world,' Lian said.

'Right then. Let's get you into this dress.'

The three of them were in some sort of a gym that had been turned over for their use. It had a bathroom and a mirror, but it wasn't exactly the sort of place a girl would choose to dress for her wedding. Despite that, Lian was glowing with happiness. Jenny felt a lump form in her throat as she watched her friend slip into the cocktail dress. Vera fiddled with Lian's hair for a moment.

'What do you think?' Lian said, twirling for their inspection.

'You look lovely,' Vera said

'No you don't,' said Jenny.

Lian's face froze.

'You need these.' From the depths of her rucksack Jenny dug out her Jimmy Choos. The ones with the totally impractical five inch heels. 'I hope they fit.'

Lian's feet were a fraction smaller than Jenny's, but it didn't matter. The shoes were the final touch to the ensemble.

'Jenny, they're fabulous,' Lian said. 'But I'll never be able to walk to the chapel. That's just a muddy track out there.'

'So you'll wear your boots as far as the porch. Then change,' Jenny insisted. 'You are not leaving a trail of muddy boot prints as you stomp down the aisle. What sort of a friend would I be to let you do that?'

When the three of them finally emerged from the gym, they found a tall straight figure in a dress uniform waiting for them outside.

'Lian,' said Captain Haugen, 'it would be my very great honour to walk you down the aisle, if you would allow me?'

'How did you know?' Lian asked.

'Word is spreading pretty fast,' the captain said with a slow smile. 'We don't get things like this happening on every cruise. I think you'll find there's quite a crowd gathered at the chapel.

He was right.

The Chapel of the Snows was a small white building topped by a short spire and a bell. As they approached, Jenny wondered if Lian would be the first bride to walk down the aisle in what must be the most remote chapel in the world. She saw other people hurrying to join them. Many of them were strangers to her — but their rough clothes and untended beards identified them as Colin's colleagues come to witness this hastily arranged wedding. Every one of them was smiling. A lot of the ship's passengers and crew had also abandoned their sightseeing to join in the celebration. She saw Eric Dempsey herding his boys into the chapel. Her boss Karl and his wife Anna had just walked inside, holding hands as they went. She looked quickly around, but there was no sign of Kit.

Jenny helped Lian change her shoes on the porch. She felt a twinge of sympathy for her friend. This was hardly the wedding of every girl's dreams. She hugged Lian, then went to take her place in the chapel. As she entered, Jenny saw Colin standing, waiting for his bride. He had procured a jacket and tie from somewhere. His face glowed with love and happiness and nervous anticipation.

Jenny felt her eyes go misty. She was wrong to pity Lian. This wedding really was incredibly romantic.

A movement to one side of the aisle caught her eye. The tiny chapel had few chairs; most appeared to have been removed to allow more people to crowd in at the back of the room. Vera had already taken a seat in the front row, saved for her by her handsome ship's doctor. Glen had found himself a seat in the second row, and was protectively guarding a spare seat next to him. He again waved to Jenny to join him. She slipped down the aisle into the seat.

'Don't you just love the stained glass window?' Glen asked.

Jenny looked up. The low summer sun was streaming through the window, lighting up the map of Antarctica worked into the stained glass. There were several colourful symbols in the window, but Jenny's eye was taken by a solitary figure on the left side.

She stifled a giggle.

'Great, isn't it?' Glen asked.

'I bet Lian never thought she'd have a penguin at her wedding,' Jenny whispered to Glen.

Under the watchful gaze of the stained glass penguin, the chaplain stepped forward.

'Could everyone please stand.'

At that moment someone hit the play button on some hidden audio system, and the sounds of the wedding march swelled through the chapel. Jenny spent a moment wondering if that had been on hand, or if someone had made a frantic dash for the internet to download it. Then other thoughts were put aside as the bride stepped through the door.

She looked amazing in the dove-grey dress, her feet encased in Jenny's reduced-price Jimmy Choos. Her face shone with utter certainty and happiness, feelings that were reflected in the face of the man who waited for her by the altar. Captain Haugen solemnly escorted Lian to her future husband's side, and kissed her cheek before placing her tiny hand in Colin's.

The short ceremony was beautiful. Jenny cried like a baby as the chaplain pronounced them man and wife.

Colin escorted a glowing Lian back down the aisle. Lian stopped to envelop Jenny in a hug.

'Thank you,' Lian whispered. Then they were moving on, as Colin's research station friends slapped him on the back and cheered raucously.

As Jenny watched them walk away, she felt someone's eyes on her. Kit was standing at the very back of the chapel, as always avoiding notice. He was the only person not looking at the happy couple. His eyes were fixed on her with an intensity that sent a shiver down her spine. She hadn't spoken to him since she and Vera had . . . Images flashed into her mind. Paintings with bright splashes of vivid colour. Paintings that hinted at a woman standing just beyond the edge of the canvas. Paintings of her?

After she'd seen the paintings in his cabin, Jenny had found a moment alone at the internet desk and had googled Kit Walker. Everything that Vera had said was true. Jenny had vague memories of seeing the story in the news, but she had been too busy trying to pass her final exams to pay any attention. Looking at the photos of Kit and his wife, Jenny had been struck by what a beautiful couple they made. How happy they both looked. There was one photo taken as he left her funeral. His face was in shadow, but his body was bowed as if broken. There was nothing after that. He had shunned the spotlight. The paparazzi hadn't been able to find him. All the media could report was the increasingly astronomical prices being paid for his work.

His work . . .

The paintings she had seen in his cabin were nothing like his earlier work. Brilliant as the early paintings had been, they lacked the wild spirit and undisguised passion of the paintings in Kit's cabin. It was as if he had discovered something deep inside himself and given it full rein. Was she in some way a part of that sudden outpouring of passion?

'Jenny?'

She started. She had been so lost in her thoughts she had forgotten Glen was by her side.

'You have been so busy with the wedding, you haven't seen anything of this place,' Glen said. He wrapped his arm around her shoulder. 'Let's go for a walk. Just the two of us.'

Jenny sought for a polite way to say no. After the emotion of the past couple of hours, she really didn't want to go with Glen. It was entirely possible he might get carried away by the mood of the moment, and that would lead to an awkwardness she would really rather avoid.

And she had a sudden urge to be alone.

Before she could answer, the long low blast of the *Cape Adare*'s horn echoed over the tiny settlement. It was time to leave.

19

It was the strangest wedding reception he had ever seen. The bride was still wearing her wedding dress, so Kit guessed this *was* a wedding reception. They were, however, lacking one important ingredient — the groom.

The party in the lounge had started as soon as the passengers had come back on board. Apparently the crew had planned a Christmas Eve party, but that had quickly morphed into a wedding reception as the ship got underway, leaving the groom back at McMurdo Station. Lian was standing in the centre of the crowd, looking at once pleased and a little lost. Kit felt a twinge of sympathy. He knew what it felt like to be alone under a spotlight that was meant for two.

Vera was with Lian. Her hands were, for once, empty of her notebook and pen and she had the ship's doctor by her side. But someone else was noticeably absent.

Kit searched the room one more time. Jenny still wasn't there.

She hadn't been on the top deck last night either. He'd waited there for a long time, no longer enjoying the solitude that he had once sought so desperately.

In the past few days, Kit had felt something he hadn't for a very long time. He was lonely. He had spent far too much time alone since Dana's funeral. He'd missed her. But he'd never felt lonely. Never wanted the company of anyone else. Until now. Those few minutes each night on the top deck with Jenny had become the most enjoyable part of his day. The most important part of his day. Those few minutes always ended far too soon. Before he had gathered the strength to say the things he wanted to say. To thank her for the incredible gift she had given him.

He turned his back on the celebration and climbed the stairs to the top deck, trying not to hope she would be there.

There was no wind, just the faint breeze caused by the ship's motion. The sun was hanging just above the horizon, turning the peaceful ocean into a molten gold mirror. She was standing at the very front of the deck, looking out over the white wilderness of ice across the golden water. Kit stood rock still, fixing the moment in his heart and soul, already knowing how he would capture this timeless moment on his canvas. His fingers ached with the need to paint. But his heart ached with the need to be with her.

He walked across the deck to take his place at her side.

Together they watched the sea and the ice. When Jenny moved, it was to look at his hands. Kit followed her glance, and saw the paint splashes on his skin.

'Ah. So you have figured it out.' It

wasn't a question.

'Vera guessed,' Jenny said. 'She kept finding sketches you'd drawn on bar napkins. Mostly guns and masked men.' She hesitated as if to say something else, but stopped before the words were formed.

Kit nodded. 'Of course. She's pretty sharp.'

'Did you know she's a famous author?'

'Yes.'

Beside him, Jenny let out a long sigh. 'It seems like I'm the only one who didn't know.'

There was a few minutes silence.

'I had to google you,' Jenny finally admitted. 'I'm not into . . . well . . . I know nothing about art. I'd never heard of you . . . Sorry.'

He shook his head. 'There's nothing to be sorry about. I never wanted to be famous. It still surprises me when people know who I am.' He hated to think of the things she might have seen on the internet. 'So now you know everything about me.'

'No. I don't,' Jenny said firmly. 'I only know what was in the papers. Tell me about you.'

Kit thought for a long moment. What could he give to Jenny that was his alone to give?

'There was this comic book I loved as a kid. The Phantom. It wasn't one of those glossy graphic novels you see now. It was simple black and white. On pretty cheap paper. But it was wonderful. The Phantom wasn't a superhero. He had no superpowers, as such. He was just a man who tried to right wrongs. That's why I went to art school. I wanted a job drawing Phantom comics. I sent them lots of drawings and pestered them for a long time.'

'That explains the sketches of guns and masked men on the bar napkins.'

'I do it all the time,' Kit said. 'Usually when I'm thinking about something else. One day some barman is going to make a lot of money selling them.'

'Did you ever get the job?'

'No. But years later, before I moved to New York, I contacted them again and offered to do a cover design for one of the comics.' The memory came flooding back and Kit began to chuckle softly. 'They said no.'

Jenny laughed too. Kit let the sound wash over him. That laugh had become the best part of his day.

'So you went on to be a famous artist. I bet they were kicking themselves for saying no.'

'I do hope so.'

The silence between them now was gentler. The air was so cold, he could see their misty breaths as they intertwined and blew away. There was so much he wanted to tell her. Perhaps it was time.

'When I was young, I sketched in black and white. Even when I started painting, those early works were in muted colours. Mostly grey. It wasn't that I had a hard childhood or anything like that. Maybe I was just naturally a bit melancholy. I seemed to see the world in grey.'

'I saw some of those paintings online. They were good.'

Kit closed his eyes. Over the years, he'd received praise and awards from many critics. Those three words coming from Jenny brought him so much more pleasure.

'I started painting in colour when I moved to New York,' he said, determined to tell her what she deserved to know. 'I met my wife there.' He hesitated, uncertain if he could continue.

'I saw her picture too. She was very beautiful.' Jenny's voice was a whisper in the twilight.

It was suddenly much easier to go on. 'She was the most beautiful thing I had ever seen in my life. I was just starting to make a name for myself. I was dragged to the ballet one night. I didn't want to go, but a big art dealer insisted I accompany her, and I couldn't afford to offend her. When I watched Dana dance, everything changed for me. I stayed up all night trying to capture her beauty. But I couldn't do it. All the paint I had was black and grey and white. I didn't have the right colours.'

Kit smiled as the good memories came flooding back.

'I went around to an artist friend at two o'clock in the morning and woke him up so he could give me the oils I needed to paint. Then I painted in a frenzy for days. Those were the paintings that finally launched my career. I sent one to Dana with an invitation to dinner. She accepted. I was already in love with her, but it took me a couple more weeks to win her over.'

Kit stopped speaking. Something was happening to him. For two years, these memories had brought with them grief and anguish. Pain and longing so strong it had almost destroyed him. But this time was different. He still grieved for the loss of his beloved wife, but the pain was not as sharp as it had been. And in the midst of his sadness, there was also some joy. For the first time since that dark, dark day, he could treasure the love he had once shared, even for such a brief time.

He felt the tears moisten his eyes.

* * *

Jenny blinked back her own tears. She could feel his grief like a tangible presence in the twilight. He must have loved her so very much. How could anyone ever replace that?

Her online search had shown her the paintings inspired by his wife. They were stunningly beautiful but at the same time, delicate and fragile. Nothing like the canvasses in his cabin below their feet.

Dana had inspired Kit to paint pale and elegant beauty. Pinks and delicate yellows. Fine strokes and elegant shapes. Who then had inspired those slashes of wild passionate colour Jenny had seen in his cabin? Was she the one? It was almost too much for her mind to grasp. She wanted to ask him, but she could not bring herself to reveal that she had invaded such an intensely private and personal a place as his art.

'I am sorry about your wife,' she said softly, reaching out to touch his paint-stained hand.

'Thank you.' His hand moved to grasp her fingers. He held her hand for just a few seconds, but it felt like an age . . . long enough to melt the icebergs or freeze the sun.

'So, now you know all about me,' Kit said. 'Tell me about Jenny Payne.'

'If you googled me, you wouldn't find anything,' she replied. 'I'm not at all important.'

'Actually, I did find you. The university site listed you as a tutor.'

She blinked back her surprise. 'I guess they haven't gotten around to taking my profile down. I only resigned a couple of days before the ship sailed.'

Jenny hesitated. Kit had opened up to her about his wife . . . should she tell him about her foolish affair with Ray?

Beside his terrible loss, her foolishness with her professor seemed so . . . unimportant. Like him, she was running away . . . hiding here on this boat. But her reasons now seemed frivolous. Her affair with Ray was nothing. She wanted to give him some part of herself that mattered.

'I come from a very big family,' she said. 'I have four brothers and three sisters.'

'You must miss them, being so far away.'

'Yes. And . . . no. At home I was always surrounded by family. Sometimes, I felt lost in the middle of it all. Don't get me wrong, I love my family and I know they love me. But with that many people in one small home . . . well . . . it can be a bit much sometimes.'

As she spoke, Jenny realised something about herself.

'I always felt a bit overwhelmed. All my brothers and sisters are brilliant in some way. Good at something. Clever.

Popular. Pretty. I guess there were times I felt a bit . . . mousey beside them.'

She heard Kit give a snort of derision. 'Don't sell yourself short, Jenny. Mousey is not a word anyone would ever apply to you.'

She was absurdly pleased by his words.

'When I signed on for this trip I'd just quit my job. I'd done something stupid. I was involved with a professor who, it turned out, was a total sleazebag. So, I ran away to sea,' Jenny chuckled. 'I guess I'm not the first to do that.'

'No. Probably not.'

'I didn't tell my family. Couldn't face them. They would all be supportive and helpful, but I didn't want that. I guess that's one of the things I've enjoyed about this trip. Having time to be myself without them. Oh!' Jenny felt a surge of panic. 'That sounds awful doesn't it? I do love them honestly. And I miss them too . . . '

'It's just nice to be your own person.'

'Yes.' Kit was right. He, who must have been so desperately alone after his wife died, understood how hard it sometimes was to be never alone.

'So, now that you have found your own place, what are you planning to do with it?'

That really was a question. One Jenny had begun to ask herself. This job had only ever been a temporary thing. A place to run and hide. But you can't do that forever.

'Well, I guess first I had better tell my family I'm not at the university any more. I thought about finding another uni, but I'm not sure that's what I want to do now.'

'What do you want to do?'

Jenny was lost for an answer. She had thought about leaving the academic world behind, but had still not decided what was going to replace it. As she sought to answer Kit's question, Jenny could feel the vague thoughts that had been hovering at the back of her mind begin to take form and substance.

'I like teaching. I always have. But teaching at uni was different to teaching here. At uni, the students wanted to learn so they could pass their exams. Here, the people just want to learn. I like that. And I am loving the places we've been visiting.'

'So, you'll sign on full time as a cruise lecturer.'

'No. But I would like to teach people about the wonderful, wild places we have. I want people to appreciate them.' As she spoke the words, Jenny realised that they were true. Her desire to stay at uni had been prompted by her feelings for Ray.

Feelings that were now so far in her past, she could barely remember what she saw in him. Instead, she was beginning to see a new direction for her interest in marine biology. 'I think I might want to work to preserve the wild places. Maybe become some sort of campaigner.' she said. 'Who would have guessed I was a tree-hugger? Here, an ocean away from the nearest tree.'

She looked at Kit, and saw the slight smile on his face. Oh God, she thought. He's laughing at me.

'I think that's wonderful,' he said. 'I envy the trees.'

He may have meant the words as a joke, but they hung in the air between them and for a very long moment, the world seemed to fade. Jenny was aware only of his handsome face, the depth of his dark eyes and the way her body seemed to sway towards him of its own accord, wanting to make a physical connection to reflect the emotions stirring her. Willing him closer. His face was just a hair's breadth from her own. She could feel his breath on her skin. If she listened, she might hear the beating of his heart — because her own heart seemed to have stopped as she waited for the touch of his lips to hers.

The ship's horn sounded — a long deafening blast that caused both of them to jump back as if burned.

'Oh, it must be midnight,' Jenny said. 'I guess that means it's Christmas Day.'

'I guess it is,' Kit said as behind him, laughing people began to appear on the deck, bringing the party with them.

'Merry Christmas, Jenny.'

The kiss was the caress of a butterfly wing. So soft she might have imagined it, but for the trembling of her heart and the ache deep inside her. She closed her eyes to savour the moment, and when she opened them, Kit was gone.

She caught a glimpse of him striding away through the crowd of revellers surging onto the deck.

'There you are,' Glen said as he appeared. 'I wanted to wish you Merry Christmas.'

Glen took her in his arms and kissed her on the lips. It was a longer kiss than the occasion technically dictated. Glen kissed her the way a man would kiss a woman he found attractive. It was a kiss full of the promise of more to come.

It was nothing.

20

There was no dawn on Christmas Day. Inside the Antarctic Circle in summer, when the sun never sets, there can be no dawn. The sun simply begins to climb back up the sky. As it did, the *Cape Adare* slid gracefully through the Ross Sea, its wake the only ripple on the surface of the still water. The ship's forward passage gradually slowed, until it came to a full stop and dropped anchor.

The whole world seemed to hold its breath. Still and silent.

On board the ship, the passengers were, for the most part still sleeping after a late night at the combined Christmas Eve party and wedding reception. The detritus of the party had been cleared away by the hotel staff and the main lounge sat empty, the Christmas tree lights glowing softly.

In the owner's cabin, light streamed in from the balcony onto an easel and a painting which almost seemed to reflect the golden glow.

There was no movement in the expedition crew quarters. The team of guides and lecturers were getting all the sleep they could before what promised to be a busy day. This was the last stop on the voyage and the passengers' last chance to set foot on the frozen continent. The turning point. At the end of the day, the sinking sun would see the *Cape Adare* heading north. The Christmas tree would be broken down before they reached the wild waters of the Southern Ocean, and then . . . home.

The only people who saw the sun begin its climb up the sky were the ship's crew. The officers and seamen whose job it was to run the ship and protect those sleeping in their beds. There were always people on the bridge, their eyes moving in a constant circle from the glowing electronic displays on the instrument panels to the big glass windows and the vista beyond.

Captain Haugen was clutching a coffee cup as he made his way onto the bridge. He greeted his watch officer and listened to his report. The captain's grey eyes swept the water. As he did, the stillness was disturbed. A whale breeched about half a kilometre from the ship. The giant creature seemed to be reaching towards the sun, wanting to be free of the ocean. Its body twisted as the leviathan fell back into the water with a mighty crash, sending water shooting into the air. In his years at sea, Captain Haugen had seen such a sight many times. But each time was as if it was the first — filling him with awe.

The captain sipped his coffee and looked at his officers.

'Gentlemen, it's going to be a good day.'

★   ★   ★

'This is your last chance to walk on the ice.' Jenny was standing by the open hatch as the seaman prepared the Zodiac for the trip to shore. 'This is one of the few places in the southern hemisphere where you are guaranteed a white Christmas.'

There was a buzz of excitement among the waiting passengers — all but two of them.

Glen Stewart and Kit Walker were standing at either side of the lobby — their eyes alternately flashing to Jenny — or to each other. For her part, Jenny was trying to ignore both of them — and failing miserably. But there was a clear difference in the way she looked at each man.

Vera wasn't one to interfere. Never that. But she felt she was already involved. Last night, she had seen Kit storm off to his room as if the devil himself was on his tail. A few minutes later, Jenny had re-joined the party, with Glen hovering by her side. That may well have been the explanation for Kit's mood. And Jenny had looked decidedly upset. Vera felt a motherly concern towards Jenny. The poor girl was so far from home and all alone, she needed someone to look out for her. She edged her way across the lobby, now packed even tighter as the group of English teenagers pushed forward, eager to get under way.

'Excuse me; do you think you could let an old lady through?'

'Yes, of course. Lads. Step back and let Mrs Horsley through.' At the teacher's command, the way across the crowded lobby magically opened up.

Bless the English, Vera thought. They have such impeccable manners.

'Merry Christmas.' Vera gave Jenny a quick kiss on the check.

'Merry Christmas,' she replied, but Vera could tell her mind was elsewhere.

'It's such a shame this is going to be our last excursion,' Vera continued brightly. 'Still, it promises to be fun.'

'Yes, it does.' Jenny raised her voice slightly. 'We'll start boarding the first Zodiac now. I just want to reiterate, this is not a settlement, as McMurdo was.

This is as wild and pristine a part of the planet as you will ever see. I want to remind you to do no damage while we are ashore. No litter. No cigarettes . . .' This was directed at the English lads and was greeted with averted eyes and soft mumbles.

'And stay close together,' Jenny continued before she stepped through the hatch into the Zodiac. 'We don't want to lose anyone.'

Vera was next through the hatch. Whereas she would normally have moved to the front of the boat to sit with Jenny, this time she chose a position near the back. She smiled sweetly at the seaman attending the engine, and waited. As she expected, Kit Walker was the next through the hatch. His eyes were firmly fixed on Jenny as he began moving towards the bow. But he wasn't the person Vera was interested in.

As soon as Glen stepped into the Zodiac, his attention turned to the front of the boat, where Kit was settling himself down next to Jenny.

'Oh, Glen,' Vera said hurriedly. 'I wonder would you mind sitting here with me,' she blinked up at him, trying to compose her face into nervous, harmless elderly lady mode. 'You being such an experienced sailor and all. Well, a woman of my years would feel so much safer with you close by.'

'But of course.' With a wistful glance in Jenny's direction, Glen moved to Vera's side.

Yes! Vera cast a quick sideways glance. Jenny was blushing slightly, trying hard to keep up a professional demeanour, while Kit sat silently beside her, his eyes hardly leaving her face. Vera could feel the tension between them.

She mentally nodded. Lian was now safely married and resting in her cabin. There were several days left before they made it back to Australia. Vera would see that Jenny wasted none of that precious time.

'So Glen,' Vera put a friendly smile

on her face, 'apart from the storm and the rescue and so forth, I really know nothing at all about you. Tell me everything.'

★   ★   ★

Jenny could hear Glen's voice, but she was glad he was sitting at the far end of the Zodiac talking to Vera. She didn't know how she would cope if *both* the men who had kissed her last night were sitting next to her. It was almost more than she could take with Kit sitting so close she could hear his breathing.

'Make sure you hold on tightly, Mrs Anderson,' Jenny said to one of the arriving passengers. 'The water might be calm, but we don't want to risk losing you.'

The passenger who had just settled into the boat nodded and carefully wrapped her fingers around the rope lining the edge of the boat.

Jenny risked a quick sideways glace, only to look full into Kit's brilliant blue eyes. It was like running head first into a brick wall. She felt her heart skip a beat, and her lips tingled with the memory of his kiss. But when she smiled, his lips didn't reply. Jenny was as eager as Kit obviously was to keep their private moments just that — private. But surely a smile wouldn't kill him.

Or was he already regretting last night . . . thinking it was a mistake.

Any further thought was driven from her head as Seaman Brown gave her a nod. The powerful roar of the Zodiac's engine put paid to any chance of conversation as they sped across the water towards the headland that was their destination.

In the madness of disembarking passengers from the boats, Jenny managed to separate herself from both men, but it wasn't to last long. As Karl Anders split the passengers into smaller groups for their walks on the ice, Jenny realised she was to have not only Kit but also Glen under her guidance. She was to take a party to the very top of the headland along a rough and tiring path. Possibly due to their hangovers, a lot of the passengers had decided to take a less strenuous option and stay at sea level, so Jenny set out with only a small group.

'This part of Antarctica is not inhabited at all,' she said as they started their long climb. 'Cruise ships bring visitors here — but it is otherwise untouched — except of course for the penguins.'

'I wish there were dogs and a sled,' someone complained from the rear of the group.

'Dogs are banned now,' Jenny said. 'The last ones were removed in 1994. Skidoos have replaced the dog sleds.'

'Well, I wish I had one of those . . . '

The climb was starting to get steeper. Jenny was beginning to feel the effort. On either side of her, Glen and Kit seemed to be unaffected by the cold or the exertion. Once, when she slipped, they both leaped to give her a hand.

She brushed them both off and doubled her pace to try to draw ahead of them.

They kept up. Both of them.

Jenny stomped hard on the ice, slamming each step down with increased fervour. She was mad and getting madder by the minute. And she wasn't entirely sure why, but she suspected it had something to do with being kissed — twice.

She'd come on this cruise to get away from a hopeless relationship with Ray — a cheater and a liar on whom she had wasted so much of her time and emotion.

A holiday romance, that's what she had been looking for. She could have it too. With Glen. He was a nice guy. Handsome, particularly now the bruises had faded. Fun. Open and honest — that was important. He'd been paying her a lot of attention — and his kiss last night had made a very clear offer. It hadn't been a bad kiss. Under other circumstances, she might have called it a good kiss. But last night, it had paled by comparison with that other kiss ... a kiss that had barely deserved the name yet had touched her to the very core of her being.

She couldn't just have a bit of a fling with Glen. Because she didn't want Glen. She wanted Kit Walker.

She wanted him despite the fact that he had followed her, and watched her and painted her ... which was all a bit freaky when you got right down to it. And he never told her what he was doing. Still hadn't. Those breathtaking canvasses would probably hang in important art galleries. He'd make money from paintings of her. He would no doubt sell them to hang in some stranger's home. And he hadn't told her. So much for honesty. He was as bad as Ray in his own way.

But the moments they had spent together on the upper deck had been so very special. They had shared secrets close to their hearts. They had shared the flight of the albatross. That first meeting at the lounge . . . even then they had shared something. Jenny tried not to think back to that first night on board ship, the sight of Kit in the sauna. Memories of his naked body, coming after the intimacy of last night's kiss left her . . . Well, it was a good thing they were in the coldest place on the planet.

That kiss! It hadn't even been a proper kiss. Just a peck really. A Christmas kiss. The kind of kiss you give a relative at the family gathering — because you have to.

Not much of a kiss.

The most wonderful kiss she had ever experienced.

'Jenny, careful!'

Strong fingers closed around her arm. She shook her head and looked around. She had reached the top of the headland, but was so caught up in her thoughts; she might just have walked straight off the edge into the ice-filled ocean below, had Glen not grabbed her.

'Sorry. Thanks . . . ' she muttered

and carefully removed her arm from his grasp; aware as she did that Kit was standing just out of reach, his face cold and unreadable.

Quickly gathering her wits, Jenny launched into her prepared lecture. All around her, the passengers were ooh-ing and aah-ing and the clicking of cameras was almost deafening. Jenny wished they would all go away and just leave her alone. Give her time to think. She answered questions, and acted as official photographer for group shots, all the while ignoring Kit's silence and Glen's attempts to get closer to her.

At long last, a glance at her watch told her it was over. The expedition team had been told to make sure their groups weren't late back to the landing point. Tonight, the *Cape Adare* would turn homewards. While the passengers celebrated Christmas with a big dinner and party, Jenny was seriously considering breaking the ban on staff drinking. Right now, a stiff drink sounded very appealing.

'If everyone has all the photos they need, it's time we started back down,' she said loudly, avoiding looking at either Glen or Kit. She felt a bit like a sheep dog as she mustered her group and got them headed back down the tricky slope. Glen was walking next to her, holding forth with great enthusiasm about the wonderful view, the party that night and life in general. Kit was a few steps behind, on the other side of her, saying nothing.

She wanted to shoot both of them.

'Oh! Jenny!' One of the passengers materialised in front of her. Jenny struggled to remember the woman's name, but couldn't.

'My bracelet!' The woman looked like she was about to burst into tears. 'My bracelet is gone. It must have fallen off up there.' She waved a distraught hand in the direction of the headland.

'Are you sure you had it on when you went up?' Jenny asked, mentally cursing the woman.

'Yes. My husband gave it to me this

morning. For Christmas,' the distraught woman said. Jenny remembered her now. Her husband was much older than her, and had not felt up to climbing the headland. 'I have to go back and find it.'

Jenny glanced at her watch again. By rights, she wasn't supposed to leave the passengers, and she certainly couldn't let the woman climb back up to the headland alone.

'I have to find it,' the woman wailed.

'Was it very valuable?' Jenny crossed her fingers hoping for the right answer.

'Yes. It is an antique. It's worth a lot of money. And he'll be so angry if he knows I lost it.'

'I can't let you go back,' she started to say, and was greeted by another loud wail. 'And you'd never find it. It could be anywhere.'

'No. I know where it is. I was sitting on a rock at the top of the trail, and I was showing it to one of the other women. I bet it came off then.'

Jenny vaguely remembered seeing the

two women together. She sighed. There was only one solution. But if she tried — it might solve two problems.

'Glen,' she said. 'I need you. And you too Kit. I need the two of you to stay with this group and see them safely back to the boat. I'll go back and get the bracelet. I know where it will be.'

'You can't go alone,' Kit said. 'Let Glen take them back to the boat. I'll come with you.'

Being alone with Kit was the last thing she needed right now. The second last thing she needed was to be alone with Glen. So she jumped in before he could say a word.

'No. I'll be fine. I can't allow a passenger to go back up that headland now. You two guide the group back down.'

'But . . . '

'Thank you,' said Jenny and before anyone could speak another word, she turned around and set off back up the steep slope, ignoring the effusive thanks from the distraught woman she was leaving behind.

The headland seemed twice as steep this time. Jenny was breathing heavily by the time she got to the top. When she finally paused for breath, she turned and looked back the way she had come. In the distance she could see tiny people milling around the landing site, and a couple of boats moving between the ship and the shore.

The flat area at the top of the headland bore the marks of the passengers' visit. Boot-prints in the snow would soon be eradicated by the wind. Jenny searched her memory for the picture of the women, sitting on the rocks admiring what must have been the bracelet. There! Jenny walked over to the grey boulders which had been exposed by the wind. The boulders were fairly close to the steep edge of the headland, and she shook her head in wonder that the woman had been so careless in such a place. Very carefully, one hand on the boulders for balance, she looked around. A flash of brilliance showed her where the bracelet lay, very close to the edge. Cautioning herself about safety, Jenny lay down and reached for the glint of gold and diamonds. Her fingers closed over the bracelet, and she slid backwards.

Jenny got to her feet then looked down at the bracelet. It was beautiful with a dozen or more huge diamonds glinting on gold. She could believe it was very, very expensive. What sort of a fool, she wondered, would wear such a thing on an expedition to climb a snow covered headland? Jenny secured the bracelet in one of the packets in her jacket and turned to go.

A kind of path was now visible. The snow had been packed down into hard ice by the boots of the visitors. The summer sun had done its work too. Despite the fact that temperatures were still below zero, a slick of semi-melted ice had formed on top of the path. Jenny had taken only a few steps, when her feet shot out from under her. She slid a little, arms failing for purchase, then found herself rolling off the path, toward the steepest side of the ridge. She was gathering speed as she slid towards another grey outcrop of rock.

Please — let that stop me — she thought.

Her body crashed into the rocks, and ceased moving. Jenny opened her eyes and stared down at the snow, just inches from her face. There was a stain of red marring the whiteness.

She struggled to understand why, as the gleaming whiteness begun to turn a dull grey. Then everything went black.

21

It was quite probably the best thing he had ever done.

The canvas was shining with the deep glow of newly painted oils. That gleam had always seemed to be something magical. He thought the magic had died with Dana. But he was wrong. His gift had never been more powerful. He could almost weep at the joy of it. He lifted his paint spattered hand and flexed the fingers; hardly able to believe that his own hand had done such work.

Today, for the first time, he had painted Jenny.

The other canvasses in the stateroom showed the world around her. He had painted the beauty that she brought into that world. Her presence had been a shadowy reflection on the ice. A few strands of hair on the wind. A shape in a bird's eye.

Not this time.

This time he had painted the woman he . . . what? The woman he wanted to spend the rest of his life painting. The rest of his life loving.

He would never sell this painting. It would be like selling a part of himself. It would be like selling his soul.

An image of his agent's face sprang into his mind. The man would be over the moon when he saw the collection in this cabin. And he would tear his hair at Kit's refusal to sell that painting of Jenny. Kit's work had never quite cracked the million dollar barrier. Not yet. Kit knew in his heart that the painting of Jenny could shatter that barrier and more besides.

It never would. He could never sell it — but he could give it away. After all, it was Christmas Day. For the first time since Dana's death, he wanted to celebrate the holiday. His love for Dana and his grief were not gone. There would always be a place in his heart for Dana. But there was room in his heart for Jenny too. And deep down, he knew this was what Dana — the Dana he had loved so deeply — would want for him.

Kit was half way to the door before he realised he was still holding a brush in his hand. He returned it to its proper place, wondering as he did where he would find Jenny. He had planned to wait for her at the landing point, after he and Glen had shepherded their group back down the headland. But the two of them had been ordered into the boats by one of the seamen, who said he'd bring Jenny in the next boatload. Once he was back on board, Kit was so desperate to paint, he'd vanished into his cabin in a kind of a daze and then lost track of time. He smiled. It was a long time since the passion had taken him like that. He welcomed it back like a long lost friend.

By the time Kit reached the passenger lounge, the Christmas party was in full swing. He looked at his watch and realised it was even later than he'd thought. He had obviously missed the dinner while he was painting. That was the problem with these never-ending days, there was no encroaching darkness to warn you that time was passing. He glanced out through the huge glass windows at the front of the lounge. The *Cape Adare* was moving. Heading home. Her mission accomplished. The noise and laughter inside the lounge indicated that the passengers also considered their voyage well done.

And the paint on his hands told him something about his own journey.

Kit entered the room, no longer feeling the need to hover in the background. No longer wanting to hide. He stood near the centre of the room and looked around for Jenny. She wasn't there. That was strange.

He saw Vera Horsley chatting to the ship's doctor and made his way towards her. Vera kept her finger on the pulse of the ship. She would know where Jenny was.

'No, I haven't seen her,' Vera said when he asked. 'I thought she might have been with you.'

'I haven't seen her since this afternoon. When she went . . . ' Kit's voice trailed off as a terrible thought formed in the back of his brain.

'She went where?' Vera asked.

'We were half way back down the headland. Some woman had lost her bracelet. Jenny went back to get it. She said she would take a later boat.'

'You don't think?' Vera's face froze.

'No. That couldn't happen,' Kit said, wishing he felt as confident as he sounded. Once more he looked around the room, and immediately recognised the blonde woman leaning on the bar. It took him just a couple of seconds to reach her side.

'Your bracelet,' he asked without any preamble. 'Have you got it back?'

The woman looked a little annoyed as she answered. 'No. I have not. And I think that is quite poor. That girl should have brought it back to me as soon as she came on board. I am of a mind to have strong words with the captain.'

Kit had already tuned her out. He spotted Glen just coming through the door. Much as he did not want to contemplate the thought that Jenny might have been with Glen — it was still a better option than the other fear that was growing in his mind.

Glen was alone.

'Have you seen Jenny?' Kit asked as he approached.

'No. Not since this afternoon,' Glen said. 'Look, I don't want to get caught in the middle of something here. If you and Jenny are . . . you know, that's fine. I'll back down.'

Kit nodded curtly. 'What I'm concerned about right now is where she is. I think maybe she got left behind.'

'Left behind? Where?'

'At that last landing. It doesn't look like anyone has seen her since.'

'That can't happen,' Glen said. 'We swipe on and off the boat with our key cards. I saw her do it this morning. The log would show if she hadn't swiped back in.'

'Oh! No!' The sound of Vera's shaky voice caused both men to turn.

'What is it?' Kit asked.

'I think . . . oh no. It's all my fault.'

Vera looked as if she might faint. Kit took her arms and guided her to a nearby seat.

'Tell me,' he said, crouching in front of her.

'Jenny's room key. I reset it.'

'What do you mean, you reset it?' Kit asked.

'Well, we wanted to . . . I wanted to get into your room. You seemed to be stalking Jenny. I thought it was all right because you are . . . well, who you are. But I wasn't sure. And I wanted Jenny to see . . . ' Vera's voice trailed off.

'What did you do to the key?'

'I know a bit about room key systems, I researched them for a book last year. I reprogrammed her key to let her into your cabin as well as her own.'

'But that wouldn't stop it registering her on and off the ship. Would it?'

Vera frowned. 'It might. If I did

something wrong.'

'Let's check her cabin,' Glen said. 'I'm staying in the staff quarters, so I can get us in there.'

They took the stairs. When repeated banging on Jenny's cabin door did not elicit a response, Kit felt his gut clench with a terrifying certainty.

'We have to turn back. Now.'

Banging on the door to the bridge did elicit a response, and within a couple of minutes, Kit had outlined his fears to Captain Haugen. The captain immediately called Karl Anders to the bridge. The pair had a hurried conversation while Kit stood by, trying to contain himself.

'Thank you. We will take it from here,' Captain Haugen assured him as Karl left the bridge at a brisk walk.

'Are you turning back?' Kit demanded to know.

'First we will search the ship. She could be on board. If we don't find her, then I will send a boat back for her.'

'It could be too late by then,' Kit was

shouting, but he couldn't stop himself. 'It's freezing out there on the ice. And she could be hurt. She'll think we've left her. She could do something stupid . . . like . . . like try to walk to McMurdo. If she does that we'll never . . . '

'Mr Walker. We will find her. I've already told a seaman to prepare my tender to launch. Karl will call in a few minutes, and then the boat will be away.'

'I'm going too.'

The captain shook his head. 'I can't allow that. As a passenger, your safety is paramount. I cannot allow you to leave the ship now.'

'I have to go back.'

'No. Sorry.'

Kit saw that the captain was not going to be moved on this. He turned on his heel and stormed off the bridge, Glen was close behind. As soon as the heavy door slammed shut behind them, Kit turned to Glen.

'Do you know where that tender boat is?'

'Deck six. Port side. They'll be prepping it now,' Glen said.

'I have get to get on board,' Kit said. 'And you are going to help me.'

Glen seemed to hesitate for a second, but only for a second. 'All right. Go get your heavy weather gear. Meet me on deck six.'

Unlike the inflatables, the tender boat had a solid hull, and a covered cabin. The seamen were busy preparing it for launch when Kit and Glen approached. One of the seaman made as if to stop them coming too close. Glen shouldered his way between the seaman and Kit.

'You can't go . . . ' the seaman started to say.

Kit ignored him. He brushed quickly past before anyone else could try to stop him and swung himself on board. A few seconds later, Karl Anders joined him, his face a mask of anger and anxiety.

'You have to get off this boat,' Karl said.

'That's not going to happen,' Kit told him firmly. 'I am coming with you.'

'No. You're not. I need to focus on finding Jenny. You'll only slow us down.'

'I won't. You're the one slowing us down — standing here and arguing. Let's get underway.'

'The captain's orders . . .'

'I don't give a damn about the captain's orders. It's Jenny I care about.'

Kit held the expedition leader's gaze. After a few tense seconds, Karl seemed to realise that Kit was not going to back down.

'If I let you stay, I need you to swear to me that you will follow my orders. I will not have you putting Jenny's life even more at risk.'

'I would never do that,' Kit said firmly.

'All right.' Karl still didn't look happy but turned away to order the seamen to proceed.

It seemed to take an eternity to launch the boat. Kit stayed well out of the crew's way. He was glad to see the doctor come on board, but at the same time, his presence made Kit even more fearful for Jenny.

The boat was lowered into the water with a resounding splash. As soon as the ropes were free, the seaman at the controls sent it powering away from the *Cape Adare*, which had come to a standstill. Conversation would have been difficult over the roar of the motor, but Kit wasn't in the mood to talk.

In the back of his head, the same words were pounding over and over like the tolling of a church bell.

Not again. Please, God. Not again.

22

Jenny was so cold. She lay in the darkness, shivering. Her head hurt so badly, she could barely breathe. She wondered if she was going to die — and thought that really, dying wouldn't be too bad if it stopped the man with the hammer in her head.

She opened her eyes. Her nose was pressed into something red and white. She winced as she moved her head just enough to realise she was lying on ice . . . and appeared to be bleeding. Slowly she tried to move one limb at a time. She eventually succeeded, which suggested that nothing was broken. It took an age for her to push herself into a sitting position. Once or twice, the world spun around her, but she managed to hold on to it.

She leaned against a large boulder and tried to steady her breathing. She raised one hand to gently touch her pounding forehead. Her fingertips came away bloody. Slowly she looked around. She remembered picking up that dratted bracelet. She remembered setting out for the landing site. Then . . . she slipped?

Moving slowly to prevent her head falling from her shoulders, as it felt likely to do, she looked upwards. She was lying at the bottom of a steep slope. There were scuff marks in the ice. She must have fallen and hit . . . probably the same rock she was now leaning against. She turned her head even further — and felt a stab of sheer terror. She wasn't at the bottom of the slope. She was nearer the top. Had she not hit this boulder, she would have kept sliding until . . . She looked at the freezing sea far below and shuddered.

The cold was seeping into her body. She could feel it sapping her energy. If she didn't start moving soon, she never would. But if she tried to climb that slope — and slipped again. This time she might not be so lucky. She probably shouldn't try to climb back up without help.

How long had she been here? The light was definitely lower than when she turned back up the headland. The sky had the pink and golden tinge of the lowering sun. She wasn't sure what time she had fallen — so she had no real idea how long she had been unconscious on the ice. Why had no one come? Her crewmates. Karl. Kit . . .

She shook her head slowly with indecision. The pain was bearable, but just. She had to make a decision. Should she try to climb back up to the path along the crest of the ridge or should she wait for help?

If help was coming, it was taking its own sweet time.

The longer she stayed there, the colder and weaker she would become. There really was no choice.

Very slowly and carefully, Jenny raised herself onto her knees. The world

347

spun sickeningly. She waited until it stopped. There was no way she was going to be able to get to her feet, far less stay on them long enough to walk out of here. If she even tried to stand up, she would fall into that freezing ocean. She knew that as certainly as she knew that if she stayed here, she would freeze. She felt despair begin to take her.

'*Jenny. You would fight. You'd never give up. You'd never leave someone you loved.*'

Kit's voice echoed in her head.

'Never.' She spoke the word as firmly to the empty sky as she had to Kit that night on the deck of the ship. She had promised him that she would never give up. And she wouldn't. Because just maybe that insignificant kiss, that unforgettable kiss had meant as much to him as it had to her.

If she couldn't walk, she would crawl.

When she had set out on this foolhardy venture, she had been wearing gloves. She remembered taking them off as she picked up the bracelet. She dug in her pockets and praise be to the god of fools and lovers, she found them. She pulled them on, put her hands onto the ice and eased her weight forward. She shuffled a few inches, then waited for the world to stop spinning. A few more inches, and another wait. The slope was steep, but she was going to be able to do this. It was just going to take a year. Maybe two.

She shuffled forward another few inches, taking great care not to slip. One slip and it would all be over.

Something dark and red dropped onto the ice in front of her face. Her head was bleeding, which explained why the world was spinning again. She waited for the laws of physics to regain control of her universe and shuffled another few inches up the steep slope.

Her breath was coming in short hard gasps, but she kept moving. The pain in her head brought tears to her eyes, but she kept on moving.

'*Jenny. You would fight. You'd never*

give up. You'd never leave someone you loved.'

'I won't give up,' she whispered. 'Kit . . . Do you hear me? I won't.'

The ice was slippery. She had to fight for every inch. Sometimes the ice won and she would slide back a few inches. But each time, she heard Kit's voice in her head.

She would not give up.

Her body was drenched with sweat. She was shivering with the cold. Her will was still strong, but her body was failing. She risked a glance up. The crest of the ridge seemed a million miles away. But she could hear Kit's voice — calling her forwards.

'Jenny!' How she wished that voice was real, not just a construct of her feverish mind.

'Kit!' Her voice was little more than a croak from her parched throat.

She must be dying. Going to heaven, because he was there. Reaching out his hands to her. Lifting her from the ice and folding her into the warmth of his arms. His face was the last thing she saw before the darkness took her.

* * *

'You have to let her go. Let me help her.'

Letting her go was almost beyond him, but the doctor's words rang true. Slowly Kit lowered Jenny's still form to the ground. But he couldn't totally let go. He kept her head cradled in his lap. He raised one hand as if to touch her face, but the doctor gently pushed it away, and leaned forward to examine Jenny's head wound.

As the doctor's back blocked Jenny's face from his gaze, Kit almost gave in to the despair washing over him. In his life, he had been privileged to love two very different but equally amazing women. He had lost one and the grief had nearly destroyed him. He couldn't bear the thought of losing the other.

'Help me,' the doctor ordered. He took a large square of shiny plastic from his bag. 'Wrap her in this. It will keep her warm.'

Kit did as he was told. He held Jenny tightly as the doctor started to bandage her injured head. She moaned softly, and stirred in his arms.

'Won't give up . . . ' she mumbled. 'Kit . . . I promised.'

Then she fell motionless again.

'We need to get her back to the ship,' the doctor said, rising to his feet. 'As quickly as possible.'

Karl stepped forward. The big man held out his arms to take Jenny, but Kit shook his head.

'I'll take her.' He scrambled upright and gently lifted her into his arms. He cradled her against his chest, his heart almost stopped as he heard her shallow, ragged breathing.

'It's a long steep ridge,' Karl said, gently placing his hand on Kit's shoulder. 'I'm here when you get tired. It will be faster and safer if we share the load.'

Numbly, Kit shook his head and

started walking down the treacherous ridgeline. He knew the need for haste, but measured each step as if he was walking on eggshells.

As if he carried in his arms the most precious thing in the world.

Because he did.

23

Kit hadn't slept for more than twenty-four hours. He looked like hell. He was sitting beside Jenny's bed, his body taut with tension. Watching him, Vera had the feeling he might implode at any moment. What a good thing William had suggested she drop by. She looked across the sick bay at the handsome doctor, and nodded.

She had this.

'How is she?'

Kit didn't take his eyes from the figure lying in the bed. Vera had a feeling he wouldn't really see her even if he did look up.

'She hasn't woken up yet.'

'And you haven't slept have you?'

'I want to be here when she wakes up.'

'Kit, you are dead on your feet. Why

don't you go and get some sleep. I'll stay with her.'

'No,' he said in a dull voice.

Vera had raised four children, who would, if asked, say their mother had 'the voice'. When the voice was employed, Vera's orders were followed without question. And it didn't just work on her family.

'You'll do her no good like this. Or yourself for that matter. You need to sleep.'

She could see that he wanted to fight her, but he had nothing left.

Jenny's head was swathed in a clean white bandage. Kit lifted her hand to his lips for a long moment, then placed it gently back on the bed. He got slowly to his feet, swaying slightly with exhaustion as he did.

'Go. Nothing is going to happen to her. I'll look after her for you.' Vera's voice was firm, but gentler now.

Kit nodded. 'Just for an hour,' he said in a voice hoarse with exhaustion.

'Just for an hour,' Vera agreed,

knowing full well that once Kit lay down, his body would demand he sleep for a lot longer than an hour.

He walked to the door, moving like an old man. He hesitated there, looking back towards the bed. The emotions on his face almost brought a tear to Vera's eye. She composed a firm look and waved him out the door, not entirely sure that he would make it as far as his cabin before he collapsed.

'Well done,' William said as she settled herself into the chair. 'I thought I was going to end up treating him as well.'

'You should have slipped something into his coffee,' Vera said.

'Medical ethics,' William responded with a smile. 'They do get in the way sometimes.'

Vera smiled. She did like this doctor. Then she turned her attention back to Jenny, who hadn't stirred since Vera entered the room.

'How is she? Really?'

'Really? She's exhausted. She has a

cut on her head and probably concussion. She needs to rest and she'll be fine.'

'That's good to know.'

'I was just about to make some tea. Would you like some?'

'Yes please.'

As William disappeared, Vera leaned over to pat Jenny's hand. The girl murmured something in her sleep that might have been Kit's name. Vera held her hand until she settled again.

William returned with her tea, then excused himself. Duty called. Vera reached into her bag and pulled forth her notebook and pen. A second dip into the bag produced a leather bound notebook that was as expensive as it looked. Vera was pretty good with a computer, but some things were best done with pen and ink. And in a manner suitable to the task.

She settled herself comfortably in the chair, opened the book on her lap and wrote the words Chapter One on the top of the first page.

She wasn't cold any more. She was lying on something soft. That must be a cloud, Jenny thought fuzzily. Didn't you get to lie on a cloud when you went to heaven? And she was in heaven. She knew that, because of Kit. She had frozen to death on that awful ridge, because that was where she first saw him, looking like an angel. Since then, every time she had tried to open her eyes, she had seen Kit's face. Looking down at her with such love and compassion that she wanted to cry. But before she could speak to him, she slipped back into the darkness. Being dead certainly had its disadvantages.

There was also the not inconsiderable matter of her head. It hurt. Really hurt. The headache to end all headaches. She didn't want to go through eternity with a headache.

Maybe if she opened her eyes, Kit could take away the pain.

Heaven seemed to be purple. Jenny

blinked then realised she was staring at a giant purple handbag on a chair next to . . .

She was lying in a bed. It was soft and white and warm — but definitely a bed, not a cloud.

'Jenny. You're awake.'

The purple bag vanished to be replaced by Vera, her face a mask of concern. 'It is so good to see you awake.' Vera turned and in a slightly louder voice called. 'William. She's awake.'

'Welcome back, young lady.'

Some of the fuzziness in her head was starting to fade a little.

'I'm back on the ship?'

'You are,' the doctor looked pleased. 'Now can you tell me your name?'

'Jenny Payne.'

'Good. Shall we try for the date?'

'It's Christmas Day.'

'Good enough,' the doctor said. 'Actually, yesterday was Christmas day. You have been asleep for a while.'

Jenny frowned as she tried to gather

her thoughts. 'I was on the ridge. Looking for some woman's bracelet. I must have slipped . . . '

'That's right,' Vera said. 'The ship left without you. That was all my fault. I'm so sorry. If I hadn't tampered with your card . . . all this would never have happened.'

'Now, let's not worry too much about that,' the doctor interrupted. 'Jenny, you have a head injury. It's not too bad but right now the best thing is for you to rest. I'll organise some soup. Nothing too heavy. You just relax.'

The doctor waved an admonishing finger at Vera. 'Vera, keep her company, but don't tire her out. Nothing too stressful.'

'Yes, William.' Vera sounded positively docile as she settled into the chair by the bed.

Jenny waited for the man to vanish, then spoke the word that had been foremost in her mind since she awoke. 'Kit?'

'He's the one who realised you

weren't on board. He pretty much forced the captain to send a boat back. He went too.'

'I saw his face. I think. While I was still out there.'

'He carried you back,' Vera said. 'He sat with you all last night. I sent him to get some sleep a couple of hours ago. He was exhausted.'

'He carried me back?'

'Yes. He wouldn't let anyone else take you.'

The bit of information eased the disappointment she was feeling at not having him here.

Any further conversation was halted by the arrival of a steward carrying a bowl of soup, some bread and juice. It wasn't exactly Christmas turkey with all the trimmings, but to Jenny, it was just the thing. She sipped the soup, letting Vera chatter on about the last night's Christmas party. Luckily, she didn't seem to need answers. That left Jenny free to think about what had happened. She might have died out there on the ice. And Kit had saved her. Kit had carried her back. Held her in his arms — and she had been unconscious. That seemed a terrible waste!

Gradually, Vera's voice seemed to get softer. Jenny barely felt the food tray being lifted from her lap as she slipped back into sleep.

★   ★   ★

Waking the next time was much easier. She simply opened her eyes and knew at once where she was, who she was and who the person sitting in the chair next to the bed was.

Unfortunately it wasn't the person she wanted it to be.

'Well, hello.' Lian smiled broadly. 'It's good to see you awake.'

'Are you taking turns watching me?' Jenny asked as she lifted herself slowly into a sitting position. Her head did not hurt quite so badly, nor did her limbs feel quite so much like jelly.

'Vera is having dinner. With the

doctor. You know, I think there may be something going on with those two.'

Jenny would have smiled at that, but her thoughts were elsewhere. On another two who might — or might not have something going on.

'Kit?' she asked.

'You just missed him,' Lian said. 'He was here while you were sleeping, but the doctor sent him away.'

'Why?'

'Apparently he had forgotten to eat. The doctor has banned him from coming back here for a couple of hours.'

'Oh.'

'You know, the two of you need to get your eating and sleeping cycles in sync if you plan to — well — do anything.'

Jenny almost blushed, but as she looked at Lian, a thought began to form in the back of her mind. Lian had left her home and family — not because she was running away, but because she was running to something. To the man she loved and the father of her baby.

She set out to get what she wanted, and here she was, married and so happy she glowed.

She would take a page from Lian's book.

Slowly she pushed herself into a sitting position. The room stayed where it was supposed to be. That was a good sign. She kicked back the covers and dropped her legs over the edge.

'What are you doing?' Lian asked.

'I'm making a break for it.'

'But the doctor . . . '

'You said he was having lunch. He wouldn't be doing that if I was dying. I'm fine. Look.' Jenny slowly got to her feet. The room spun just a little, a fact she was able to hide from Lian. 'See. I'm fine. I'm going to Kit.'

'Like that?'

Jenny looked down at herself. Lian had a point, she was wearing some sort of cotton hospital style nightie. And yes, now that she thought about it, it did gape at the back.

'I need clothes,' she said. They would

need to be warm ones too, because she knew exactly where she would find Kit.

'I'm really not sure about this,' Lian said.

'I am. I wonder if my clothes are here anywhere?' Jenny took a step from the bed, and the room started spinning again in a manner she couldn't hide. She reached for the bedhead to steady herself.

'Stay put,' Lian said. 'I'll look.'

A quick search revealed Jenny's shoes and jeans. Her jacket showed signs of having blood hastily removed. But of her T-shirt, there was no sign.

'They must have thrown it away,' Jenny said. 'I guess there was too much blood on it.' Which didn't help her at this moment. She looked at Lian. The girl was smaller than Jenny, but she was pregnant and . . .

'Can I borrow your top?'

'What?'

'I can hardly walk around wearing this,' Jenny tugged at the hospital gown. 'I need a shirt. Please!'

Lian hesitated. 'But the doctor said you need to rest.'

Jenny shook her head. 'Doctors don't know everything.'

24

He was there, of course. Right where she knew he would be. Standing on the top deck in the spot she had come to think of as theirs. The sun was very low in the sky, and there were clouds gathering. The beautiful pink and golden light had been left behind as the *Cape Adare* worked her way north. The greyness of the evening seemed to hover around Kit's shoulders.

Jenny steeled herself emotionally and physically, and started to walk across the deck. She had almost reached Kit, when he heard or sensed her. Slowly he turned around. The darkness in his eyes tore at her heart. But then his face changed. His eyes glistened as he closed the distance between them and took her in his arms. His arms were strong. His body was warm. And as she laid her head on his chest, she could almost feel the beating of his heart.

For a long time they stood like that.

Finally, Kit brushed a kiss across the top of Jenny's head, and released her. Not entirely. He kept his arm around her shoulders as they stepped up to their usual place — side by side at the ship's rail, looking out over the ocean.

It was Kit who finally broke the silence.

'I thought I had lost you.' His body was taut with emotion. His journey to this place had been long and painful. Jenny knew it wasn't quite over.

'Kit, tell me how Dana died.'

'We were going to have a baby.' His voice broke. 'Oh, God. We were so happy. Dana stopped dancing as soon as she learned she was pregnant. Having a baby would have pretty much ended her career, but she didn't care. She . . . we wanted the baby so much.'

He choked on the words. Jenny barely dared to breathe as she waited for him to say what he needed to say.

'She was such a strong dancer, but

weak in other ways. She lost the baby.'

Jenny put her hand over his on the railing. The grief in his voice was palpable.

'When she came home from hospital she just sat there. She barely spoke. She wouldn't talk to her friends. They were all dancers, you see. Dancing at that level is so hard on a woman's body. She thought she was to blame. I tried to help her, but she was so distant. She wouldn't talk to me. She would barely look at me. So, I buried myself in my studio.'

'You were grieving too,' Jenny whispered.

'I should have been there for her. One day, she was just gone. We were living in Manhattan — on the upper west side. The doorman at our apartment told me she had gone towards the park. Central Park is a pretty big place. I searched for hours. She was dead when I found her. The doctors said she had taken a massive overdose.'

Tears pricked at Jenny's eyes for this

desperately sad woman whom she had never met. 'I am so sorry.'

'It was my fault. I should have been there. I was in my studio painting when she decided she wanted to die. If I had been with her . . . '

'This is not your fault, Kit. It was a tragedy but it was not your fault. You have to know that.'

'I felt so guilty, but I was angry too. At her. She just gave up and left me. She wasn't willing to try. To fight for us . . . '

Kit took a long slow breath.

'After the funeral, I went into the studio. I picked up a brush. And there was nothing. I couldn't paint any more. There had always been a darkness inside me, Jenny. Dana softened it. Gave it some colour. I fell back into the darkness when she died. And, ashamed as I am to admit it, there were times I thought I wanted to die too.'

'That's not why you came on this cruise is it?' Jenny asked, fear in her voice. 'You weren't thinking of . . . '

'Honestly, Jenny, I don't know. I've spent the last year travelling. Always taking my tools with me. I've been to the most beautiful places. Seen so many different cultures and people. I desperately wanted to believe one of them would inspire me to paint again. Nothing did. Until I saw you — you brought new colour into my life. Bright, wonderful colours. Living . . . loving colours.'

Jenny smiled through her tears. 'Love at first sight?' she said, trying to keep her voice light, despite the fact that her heart felt like it was going to explode.

'It seems to be my way,' Kit said ruefully. 'I remember the exact look on your face when the Coke can exploded in the library. That was quite some first sight.'

'I have a confession to make,' Jenny said. 'It wasn't my first sight of you.'

'Really?'

'Our first night out. You were . . . um . . . you were in the sauna.'

'The sauna?' Kit raised an eyebrow. 'I

thought I saw someone. That was you?'

Jenny nodded, blushing furiously.

Kit laughed. It was a rich, happy sound that Jenny knew she would never tire of hearing.

'Then I must make a confession too,' he said. 'I saw you that day with the dolphins. Talking to them. That was the day I first felt the desire to paint again. That was the day you gave it back to me.'

'It was always in you, Kit. You just had to find it. And speaking of finding things,' Jenny said with a start. 'I wonder . . . ' She reached into the pocket of her jacket and her fingers closed around something cold and metallic. The bracelet shone dully in the lowering light when she pulled it out of her pocket. 'I suppose at some point I should give this back.'

'That stupid bracelet. I almost lost you because of that. I want to throw it in the ocean.'

'It's too pretty,' Jenny said. 'Let's give it back.'

'You have to promise me you will never do something that stupid ever again.'

'I can't do that,' Jenny said, feeling him tense beside her. 'That's the person I am. I sometimes do stupid things. I will make mistakes and fall down. You can't wrap me in cotton wool, Kit. But,' she turned to look at him, holding his face between her hands as she spoke with all the feelings pouring through her heart. 'I promise you this, Kit Walker. I will never give up. I will always fight my way back. To you. For you. For us. Even if I have to do it on my hands and knees.'

Jenny was never sure if she kissed Kit, or if Kit kissed her. It was a kiss that lasted a very long time.

Jenny shivered as they broke apart.

'You're cold,' Kit said. 'You shouldn't be out here. Let's go down to my stateroom. There's something there I want to show you.'

'Ah. I may have seen it. There is this small matter of a break-in I have to explain . . .'

Kit was chuckling again as they made their way across the open deck. His arms stayed around her shoulders. Not so much to help as to just keep her near him. She would be very happy to live with that for a lifetime or two.

As Jenny and Kit disappeared into the ship, just as the sun dipped below the horizon, two shapes slipped beneath the clouds. The two great albatross soared easily on the winds, pacing the ship for a short time, before turning on the wind to continue their lifelong journey together.